ON THE ROPES

While Frank gasped for breath on the mat, he saw Jimmy Roman slam Joe on the side of the head with a blow from his forearm.

Joe went down hard, and the Romans tossed him into the ropes, twining them around his arms so he was hopelessly tangled. Frank desperately tried to get up, but Victor slammed him back down to the mat with a two-fisted ax-handle punch.

Before Frank could make any countering moves, he felt Victor pick him up around the waist and hold him upside down. Then he saw Jimmy Roman climb up to the top of the corner post. It looked as if Jimmy was getting ready to fly through the air.

In a flash of realization that sent chills through his body, Frank knew he was being set up for a spiked pile driver, an illegal move that could break his neck!

Books in THE HARDY BOYS CASEFILES® Series

Available from ARCHWAY Paperbacks

CHOKE HOLD

FRANKLIN W. DIXON

AN ARCHWAY PAPERBACK
Published by POCKET BOOKS

New York   London   Toronto   Sydney   Tokyo   Singapore

AN ARCHWAY PAPERBACK *Original*

An Archway Paperback published by
POCKET BOOKS, a division of Simon & Schuster
1230 Avenue of the Americas, New York, NY 10020

Copyright © 1991 by Simon & Schuster
Produced by Mega-Books of New York, Inc.

ISBN: 0-671-70048-0

First Archway Paperback printing May 1991

10 9 8 7 6 5 4 3 2 1

THE HARDY BOYS, AN ARCHWAY PAPERBACK and colophon are registered trademarks of Simon & Schuster.

THE HARDY BOYS CASEFILES is a trademark of Simon & Schuster.

Cover art by Brian Kotzky

Printed in the U.S.A.

IL 7+

Chapter

1

"GIVE UP, FRANK! You're beaten!" Joe Hardy said, his blue eyes flashing as he tightened his hold on his older brother.

"Never!" Frank replied through gritted teeth. He strained against Joe's viselike hammerlock.

Joe thought he and Frank were about evenly matched in terms of strength, but Frank was slightly quicker.

Frank's speed wouldn't help him this time, though. Joe bore down on his older brother, forcing his shoulders closer to the mat. Frank tried to kick out with his legs, but he couldn't dislodge Joe.

"Don't let him pin you, Frank," a cheerful voice called from outside the ropes of the wrestling ring. "Come on! You can do it!"

1

"Hey!" Joe called to the man coaching Frank. "Whose side are you on, Sammy?"

Sammy Rand, better known to his fans as the Kung Fu King, was a compact, heavily muscled man whose straight black hair hung down to his shoulders. He was dressed in a gold-colored muscle T-shirt, black sweatpants, black kneepads, and wrestling boots.

His almond-shaped brown eyes sparkled as he shrugged his broad shoulders and smiled. "Fair's fair, Joe. Since you're on the Bayport High wrestling team, I know you're a better wrestler than Frank."

"Sammy, if you've got any suggestions to avoid getting pinned, I could use one right about now!" Frank panted.

"It won't do you any good, anyway, Frank. You're licked!" Joe said as he shoved Frank's shoulders down to the mat. "One, two, th—" Joe didn't finish his count.

With catlike quickness Frank kicked out and got to his feet. He faced Joe in a combat crouch, knees bent, hands ready.

"Brace your feet wider, Frank!" Sammy called. "And next time Joe gets you down, take a deep breath and really expand your chest. Flex your shoulders in and out quickly to keep him from getting a good grip on you."

Joe circled his opponent, trying to size up the situation. Although Frank was an inch taller, Joe thought that his extra weight would be an advantage.

Joe feinted left with his head. Frank moved to counter this, but Joe stepped inside, sweeping Frank's left foot out from under him. At the same time he grabbed Frank and shoved him backward.

Frank fell to the mat with a bone-jarring thud. But before Joe could pin him, Frank inflated his chest and flexed his shoulders and wriggled free of Joe's grasp. Then Frank grabbed one of Joe's arms and twisted it behind his back and shoved him into the mat.

"Time!" Sammy called. "You guys are looking good," he commented as the brothers walked toward him. "And with a little more work, Frank, I think you could take Joe. You've always been quick. After all, you were one of my best karate students back home in Bayport."

"Thanks, Sammy," Frank said as he stepped through the ropes and drank from the jug of ice water Sammy held out. Joe was right behind his brother, taking the water jug and draining it in two gulps.

"After you guys catch your breath, how about spotting for me while I do my free-weight workout?" Sammy suggested.

"Sure, Sammy," Frank agreed, pushing his dark hair off his face.

"And maybe then you'll explain why you

3

wanted us to come out here to Allentown, Pennsylvania, posing as wrestlers," Joe said.

"I've got my reasons," Sammy replied, walking to a weight bench and sitting on it. "Joe, is anybody close enough to overhear us?"

Joe scanned the cavernous interior of the International Wrestling Association training center. He noticed a pair of wrestlers rehearsing their moves in each of the three wrestling rings that were located in the center of the room. And at the far end of the gym several wrestlers were on the mats, stretching and practicing falls.

As he checked out the area, Joe wondered what Sammy was worried about. Joe and Frank had known Sammy since he had been Frank's karate instructor in Bayport. Joe thought about how in a few short years Sammy had gone from being an obscure martial arts teacher to one of the most successful wrestlers in the country.

Joe turned back to Sammy and sat down on a mat next to his brother. "Coast is clear. No one's close enough to overhear us. Now, what gives, Sammy? Why all the precautions?"

"I'm more than a little curious now myself," Frank added. "You said you needed us to investigate a problem for you." Sammy was well aware of the Hardys' reputation as detectives, which was why Frank assumed he had called them.

"I'm in trouble, guys," Sammy said quietly. "You remember that bout I had with Major Disaster about three months ago?"

"The one where he creamed you with a chair?" Joe responded. "I saw that. I can't believe Disaster got away with it!"

"Yeah, well, the chair was supposed to be a breakaway, made of balsa wood, so he could hit me with it without hurting me, but somehow a real one got substituted. When he hit me, I went down for real. That little mishap resulted in four cracked ribs. I was out of commission until a couple of weeks ago."

"Do you think Disaster switched the chairs?" asked Frank.

"I didn't at first," Sammy answered. "The Major and I had choreographed our moves ahead of time like pro wrestlers do for every bout. So I thought he'd made an honest mistake and grabbed the wrong chair. Disaster's no mental giant, you know."

"What changed your mind?" asked Joe.

"I started to suspect Disaster a couple of weeks ago, when I got into the ring for the first time after my 'accident' for a little training session."

"What happened?" Joe prompted.

"I took a break and went for a drink of water, but as I raised my bottle up, it smelled funny. When I checked it, I found out it was filled with ammonia. Somebody had to have put it in there deliberately.

"So I started to think," Sammy continued, "that since Disaster didn't permanently knock me out of commission with the chair, he might be trying to get me again."

"Did you do anything about it?" asked Frank.

"Sure," Sammy replied. "I went to Stanley Warfield, the International Wrestling Association president, and told him about both incidents. But he said they were just accidents and refused to do anything. That was when I decided to call you guys."

Sammy sighed. "Like I don't have enough other problems now. Daniel East, who runs the TV network that broadcasts all the bouts put on by the National Association of American Wrestlers, the IWA's main competition, has been after me for weeks to switch to the NAAW.

"When I finally gave him a definite no last week, he got really mad. Warfield told me East tried to sell his operation to him after I turned him down. Warfield refused his offer and got the same kind of reaction I did from East.

"Anyhow," Sammy continued, "that's the least of my problems right now. I need you guys to help me nail whoever is responsible for these 'accidents.' ''

"Glad to help, Sammy," Joe assured him.

The worried expression on Sammy's face left as he broke into a wide grin. "Great! I knew I could count on you guys. I've already started telling the other wrestlers that you two are trying to break into the biz and are acting as my assistants."

"Sounds good," Frank commented. "That should give us freedom to check around without arousing any suspicion."

Suddenly a hoarse bellow cut the air inside the training center. "Kung Fu, you better drag your sorry tail into that workout room and get in shape! You're going to need it to avoid total humiliation on Saturday!"

Startled, Joe turned in the direction of the voice and saw Major Disaster, the IWA's number-two wrestler and resident bad guy. He was standing near the entrance of an adjoining workout room. Disaster was a big burly man whose brown hair was shaved in a military crew cut. Joe guessed that his battered nose had been broken more than once. Disaster was clad in baggy camouflage pants, a khaki T-shirt, and brown wrestling boots. The lights overhead gleamed off his mirrored sunglasses.

The next person Joe noticed was a petite, blue-eyed, blond woman standing at Disaster's side. She was dressed in a tight royal blue jumpsuit, with a long blue feather boa.

"Who—" Frank began, but Sammy cut him off.

"That's Major Disaster," Sammy said out of the corner of his mouth.

"Who's his blond sidekick?" Frank wanted to know.

"She's Marvelous Missy Mayflower, Disaster's manager," Joe replied as Sammy stood up and turned to face Disaster.

"Disaster, you windbag—if that's the best you can do, you'd be better off letting Missy get in the ring with me Saturday. I'll tie you up in knots, you brass-plated phony!"

"Why wait for Saturday, creep?" Disaster shouted, taking a step toward Sammy. "We can settle it right here! Right now!"

"Come on, Major—save it for the paying customers," Missy said, grabbing Disaster's arm and trying to drag him toward an exit.

"I'm ready any time, you wimp! I'll stuff that championship belt down your throat!" Disaster shouted over his shoulder as Missy did manage to pull him away.

As soon as the door swung shut behind Disaster and Missy, Sammy turned to the Hardys. "That guy's had it in for me ever since I won the IWA championship two years ago. I really don't trust him or Missy."

"Then checking out Disaster and Missy is

a good place to start our investigation," Frank observed. "What's the Major's real name?"

"Fred J. Stone," Sammy replied.

"Gee, Missy looks pretty trustworthy to me," Joe interrupted with a devilish grin.

Before Frank could reply, he noticed Slim Sorkin, Sammy's trainer, approaching. Although Slim stood about an inch taller than Frank's six-one, Frank guessed that Slim weighed about fifty pounds less than he did. Slim's big brown eyes seemed to pop out of his gaunt face, and his dark hair fell straight and flat against his head.

"Sammy!" Slim shouted. "Get into the workout room. You've got to get into shape for your next two bouts."

"What are you working on next, Sammy?" asked Joe.

"Upper arms," Sammy replied. "I think I'll do some rope climbing in the V position. That way I can work on my arms and my abdominals at the same time."

"Want us to time you?" Frank asked.

Smiling, Sammy shook his head. "Not the first time," he replied. "I've felt really out of shape since my ribs got hurt. I'll probably be slow as molasses."

"I'll get you into shape, Sammy. Never fear," Slim said seriously. "Come on." Sammy and the Hardys followed him to the workout room.

Sammy grabbed the thick rope dangling from the ceiling of the workout room and stuck his legs out in front of him at a forty-five-degree angle. Joe was amazed at how easily Sammy pulled himself up the rope. And he was fast!

"If that's being out of shape, I'd hate to see Sammy when he's in shape," Joe commented to his brother.

Frank glanced at the second display on his digital wristwatch. "Ten seconds to the top," he observed. "Not bad for someone who just came off the disabled list."

Joe glanced at the top of the rope, to watch Sammy. Just below the hook that attached the rope to a support beam, the rope was unraveling!

"Sammy—the rope's going!" Joe shouted.

Frank raised his eyes, and for a moment his heart stopped. Strands of rope were popping one after another. In another second Sammy would plunge to the floor!

Chapter

2

FOR A SECOND Frank thought Sammy was doomed, but the wrestler's lightning reflexes saved him. His hands shot up and wrapped around the beam the hook was screwed into.

Frank heard Sammy grunt with pain as he grabbed the beam. Frank guessed the sudden jarring had sent a shock of pain through Sammy's healing ribs.

"Help me, guys—I can't hold on long!" yelled Sammy.

"We'll figure out something!" shouted Joe.

Frank scanned the room for a ladder to climb to reach Sammy. Nothing. Frank watched as Joe rushed over to a tall pile of wrestling mats stacked in one corner. Slim followed Joe to the mats.

"If we stack these mats up high enough,

Sammy will have something to break his fall!'' Joe shouted, grabbing two mats and dragging them to a spot directly under Sammy.

"I don't know about this," Slim said doubtfully as he grabbed the opposite ends of the mats Joe was dragging. "It's a long shot."

"It's the only shot we've got." Joe turned and ran back to the pile of mats.

"I'm slipping!" Sammy shouted desperately. "Hurry, guys. Hurry!"

Realizing that they would never get enough mats piled up in time, Slim ran to the doorway of the workout room and cupped his hands around his mouth. "We need everybody's help! Hurry! Sammy's in trouble!"

Joe was throwing another mat onto the pile when a dozen wrestlers and trainers came pouring into the room. In moments the pile of mats was two feet high.

"There's a big stack of mats under you, Sammy. Let go and just go limp when you fall!" Frank instructed.

"Here goes nothing!" Sammy shouted. He released his grip on the beam. Sammy fell backward with his arms and legs spread wide and landed in the center of the pile with a muffled thump.

Frank, Slim, and Joe rushed to Sammy's side. Sammy had the wind knocked out of him, but otherwise he seemed unhurt.

"How're your ribs?" Slim asked as he helped Sammy to sit up.

"Okay. They're okay," Sammy gasped. He sat on the edge of the stack of mats to catch his breath. The other wrestlers and trainers tried to crowd around Sammy, but Joe kept them back.

"All right, everybody, back off. Give Sammy room to breathe," ordered Joe.

"Thanks for your help, folks," Frank announced. "The rope broke, but Sammy's okay." Slowly the crowd began to disperse.

"I'll tell the maintenance boys about this rope," Slim volunteered. "I'll be back in a little while."

"That was close," Sammy said to the Hardys after Slim left. "If it hadn't been for you guys, I would've been splattered all over the floor."

"I'm just glad we were here," Frank said, shooting a quick look up at the frayed stump of rope hanging from the beam. "I think this is another of those 'accidents' you were telling us about."

"Major Disaster and Missy Mayflower were the last ones in this room," Joe said. "Do you think they could have cut the rope?"

Sammy shrugged. "Disaster hates me, but I don't know if he hates me enough to kill me."

"Maybe Disaster wants to be the IWA

champion more than you know. Maybe enough to try to kill you," Joe suggested.

"I've wrestled against him many times, but I don't really know the guy. He's a very private person," replied Sammy.

"I'll do a background check on him," Frank said, whipping out a small notebook.

"What about Missy? Any reason other than Disaster for her to want to hurt you?" asked Joe.

"Well," Sammy said slowly. "If you remember some wrestling history, Joe, the name Mike Mayflower should sound familiar."

"Mike Mayflower," Joe said excitedly. "Sure, Mike Mayflower, one of the first wrestling superstars! You mean Missy's—"

"His daughter," Sammy finished. "And Missy might be out to get me because of her brother, Mitch."

"Why? What happened with Mitch?" asked Frank.

"Two years ago, Miracle Mitch Mayflower was the IWA champ. I took away his title belt in our first match. During the match Mitch tore some ligaments in his knee and had to retire from wrestling."

"And you think Missy blames you for ruining his career?" asked Joe.

"I'm sure of it," Sammy said quietly. "Before that match, Missy was friendly to me. Ever since Mitch got hurt, she won't give me the time of day."

"Well—" Frank began, but his sentence was cut off by a loud commotion coming from the next room.

With Sammy in the lead, the Hardys went out into the huge, brightly lit gym of the IWA training center.

In one corner of the room, near the main entrance, Frank spotted a television camera crew clustered around a muscular black giant decked out in a snakeskin jacket, pants, and cowboy boots. Standing next to the giant was a smaller, older man.

"Oh, no! Warfield's going to go through with that challenge promo. I thought I convinced him to drop it," Sammy said angrily.

"Who's the big guy?" asked Frank.

"That's my buddy Ethan Berry. He's known in the ring as the Constrictor. He's one of my chief rivals, and the IWA's most popular 'bad guy.' We're actually best friends, but the fans don't know that."

"What do you mean by 'bad guy'?" Frank asked.

"In professional wrestling you're either a good guy or a bad guy," Sammy explained. "We choreograph most of the moves ahead of time so that sometimes the good guy wins and sometimes the bad guy wins."

"You mean wrestling matches are fixed?" Frank asked in surprise.

"It's all show biz! Now I have to go over and listen to the Constrictor bad-mouth me. Then I've got to sound off at him. It's to publicize our bout for a week from Saturday."

"And who's the older guy standing next to Constrictor?" asked Joe.

"That's Stanley Warfield, the IWA president—the guy who's making me go through this," answered Sammy.

Joe studied Warfield and thought that he had probably been a good athlete when he was younger. But he'd let his body get out of shape now. Warfield was almost completely bald, except for a neatly trimmed fringe of dark hair around his shiny dome. The hairiest parts of his head were his thick mustache and bushy eyebrows.

Joe's thoughts were interrupted as the Constrictor grabbed a microphone and began to speak.

"I'm here to challenge the IWA's so-called champion, the Kung Fu King, to wrestle me for the undisputed IWA championship! He doesn't deserve to be called champion! I'm calling you yellow, Kung Fu! I'm saying you're afraid to face the awesome might of the Constrictor!"

Frank saw Sammy take a deep breath and

angrily stalk across the gym toward the Constrictor.

"Constrictor, I'll wrestle you anywhere, any time. You're nothing but an overrated loudmouth!"

The camera crew quickly wheeled around and trained their camera on Sammy.

Sammy stalked up to within a foot of the Constrictor and yelled, "You hear me, punk? I'll throw you out of any ring you're stupid enough to enter with me!"

"You think I'm afraid of a wimp like you?" The Constrictor lunged at Sammy.

Stanley Warfield stepped between the two wrestlers to prevent any punches from being thrown.

Frank observed that a large crowd had gathered. Wrestlers had stopped their practices to witness the confrontation. Trainers in warm-up clothes and managers in rumpled suits moved forward to watch the shouting match between Sammy and the Constrictor.

Frank also noticed that Missy Mayflower and Major Disaster had come back and joined the crowd. Disaster's expression was unreadable behind his mirrored sunglasses, but Missy looked as if she was enjoying the show.

Suddenly Frank felt Joe jab him in the ribs with his elbow. Joe gestured with his head toward a different part of the crowd.

"Take a look over there, Frank. Check out

the short guy standing next to the big dude in black with the sunglasses."

"Who are they?" asked Frank.

"The short one's Daniel East, president of East Broadcasting Corporation. The big one is the Living Weapon, the NAAW's top wrestler."

"But what are they doing—" Frank started to ask, then stopped as he saw Disaster leave the training center.

"Disaster's splitting. I want to tail him to see where he's going. It might be a lead," said Frank.

"Good idea," Joe agreed. "I'll stay here and keep an eye on Missy and East."

Frank gave Joe a knowing look. "I had a feeling you were going to say that. Let Sammy know that I'm borrowing his car, okay? I'll leave the van for you."

Joe nodded and walked over to where Sammy and the Constrictor were hurling insults at each other. Stanley Warfield stood watching, his arms folded, and seemed to be pleased with something.

Frank ducked out a side exit of the training center and ran around to the parking lot. He hoped he'd be able to catch up with Disaster.

Just as Frank reached the parking lot, he spotted Disaster climbing into a black sports car. Frank hopped into Sammy's red convertible and felt under the dash for the spare key hidden there. He quickly started the car and took off after Disaster.

Disaster drove fast, weaving expertly in and out of traffic. Frank kept on his tail for about twenty minutes. They passed through the center of Allentown and then into an area across from a railroad track where the streets and buildings looked run-down. As he drove, Frank noticed nothing but dilapidated office buildings and stores, many of which were boarded up with For Rent signs nailed to their doorframes.

After driving a few blocks in this neighborhood, Disaster made a left turn and pulled into a parking lot. Frank noted that the parking lot was next to the tallest building on the block. I wonder where he's going? Frank thought.

He drove slowly past the parking lot, watching as Disaster got out of his car and walked through a back entrance of an office building.

Frank parked his car around the corner and made his way back to the building through broken bottles and other trash.

As he neared the rear entrance of the building, Frank heard what sounded like a conversation coming from behind the window next to the doorway. Frank stole up to the grimy window and tried to peer inside. The window was too filthy even after Frank wiped some of the dirt off with a piece of newspaper. The window was as filthy on the inside as the outside.

As Frank crept up to the next window, he heard the distinctive sound of glass being crunched somewhere behind him.

He started to turn his head, but an iron grip on his neck held him in place. He couldn't shake it free. Then he felt his body being slammed into the brick wall with amazing force!

Chapter

3

As Joe walked up to the edge of the small crowd surrounding Sammy and the Constrictor, he noticed that Daniel East and the Living Weapon had been joined by two other men. Joe recognized the guys as the Roman brothers.

Like the Constrictor, the Roman brothers were bad guys. The two men were almost identical, except that one of them stood two inches taller than his brother. The shorter one had a scar on the left side of his chin. Both men had dark wavy hair cut in the style that reminded Joe of ancient Roman sculptures. I get the feeling I'll be seeing more of those guys, Joe said to himself.

Joe then turned back to watch Sammy's confrontation with the Constrictor.

"Get out of my way, Warfield. Let me tear his head off!" the Constrictor shouted.

"Easy, big guy," Warfield said, his fleshy face gleeful. "You'll get your chance. Just wait till you meet in the ring."

"That's right, Kung Fu, wait till we meet in the ring. But I'll tell you right now, you don't stand a chance against me, you little nothing!"

"That's just like you. Your mouth against my muscle. Do you think I take a third-rater like you seriously, Constrictor?"

"Third-rater! Why you—" The Constrictor lunged at Sammy over Warfield's shoulder.

"Go ahead, Constrictor, knock his block off!" Joe heard a female voice shout. "I'd like to see that, in the ring or out of it!"

Joe swiveled around to see Missy urging on the Constrictor. Her pretty face was now twisted in hate. Her hostility toward Sammy was very obvious.

"Kung Fu, I'm going to lay such a hurting on you that you're going to have to retire—in a wheelchair!" the Constrictor shouted.

"Yeah? We'll see about that, pinhead," Sammy retorted. "In the meantime, I can stay in the company of a loser only so long, so I'm going back to my dressing room. I'd advise you to leave now before I throw you out."

"You and what army, punk?" the Constrictor snarled back.

Sammy ignored the last of the snakeskin-clad wrestler's threats. Turning, he sauntered across the gym toward his dressing room.

Joe saw Warfield give the cut signal to the camera crew, and they turned off their lights and camera. The fun was over, and the crowd began to break up.

As he turned to follow Sammy into his dressing room, Joe heard Warfield call, "That's a wrap!"

Joe looked around for Daniel East and the Living Weapon, but they had disappeared.

"Hey, Sammy, wait up!" Joe called after him.

Sammy stopped long enough for Joe to catch up. When he reached the big wrestler's side, he noticed that Sammy was seething.

"What's wrong, Sammy?" asked Joe.

"I'm still mad at Warfield for making me go through with this challenge promotion with the Constrictor," Sammy replied, barely controlling his anger. "You'd think he'd give me a break after today with the rope snapping and all. But not him! He'll do anything for a buck and publicity."

Sammy threw open the door to his dressing room and angrily kicked over a folding chair just inside. Joe followed him and watched Sammy pace back and forth in front of a large mirror lined with light bulbs.

Joe slowly took in the dressing room. The

wall to the right of the door was lined with three tall metal lockers containing Sammy's wrestling costumes and workout clothes. A TV, VCR, and small cabinet filled with videotapes sat in the far corner of the room beneath a poster from Sammy's campaign against steroids. Joe recalled how Sammy had toured the country lecturing on the dangers of steroids.

"I've got enough to deal with, with somebody trying to wreck my career and maybe kill me! I don't think it's fair to make me go through with those stupid promos. Warfield doesn't even believe I'm in danger!"

"Take it easy, Sammy! Frank and I are going to help," Joe reminded him.

Sammy drew a long breath and collapsed into a padded leather swivel chair. "Yeah, you're right, Joe, I've got to calm down. Sorry I lost my temper," Sammy said quietly.

"Forget it. Anybody would get a little freaked out after what happened with the rope," Joe said sympathetically.

Joe picked up the chair Sammy had kicked over and sat down in it a few feet from him. Spotting a pad of paper and a pencil on the counter, Joe picked them up and began making notes.

"The important thing now is to figure out who our main suspects are. Once we have a list of suspects, we'll investigate to find out who has the strongest motive for knocking you out of the business," Joe told Sammy.

"You should probably start with Missy Mayflower and Major Disaster. I don't think Major hates me enough to kill me, but he doesn't exactly like me, either. And I think Missy could be capable of just about anything—maybe even murder," Sammy said.

"It's hard to think that someone as young as Missy could be a killer," Joe said dubiously.

"Don't let that sweet face of hers fool you, Joe. Missy may be only nineteen years old, but she's one tough customer. Here, let me show you what I mean."

Sammy walked over to the VCR and searched through a stack of tapes. After a few seconds he pulled one out. "This is a tape of the match where I got hurt. Watch," he instructed as he popped the tape into the VCR.

Joe watched as Sammy fast-forwarded the tape and stopped it. Then he ran the tape at normal speed, and Joe watched as Missy handed a wooden folding chair to Major Disaster. Disaster grabbed it, then charged forward, slamming Sammy in the side with it. Joe winced as he watched Sammy crumple to the mat, his face contorted with pain.

"Ow, that hurts just to look at it," Joe commented.

"That move was all worked out before the

match," Sammy explained. "It was supposed to be a breakaway chair."

"So you think Missy probably substituted the real chair before the match?" Joe asked, quickly scribbling notes.

"Someone did. I sure wouldn't put it past her. She blames me for what happened to her brother. And I think she'd stop at nothing to make sure that I have to quit wrestling like he did."

Sammy had picked up the remote control device and was automatically rewinding the tape when Joe said, "Run the tape back to the point just before Missy hands the chair to Major.

"Sammy—freeze that frame!" Joe shouted excitedly. He stood up so fast his own chair toppled backward. "Look there!" he said, pointing to the upper portion of the screen. Joe and Sammy watched as a pair of hands moved a folding chair into position just before Missy grabbed it.

Joe hit the Rewind button on the VCR and ran the tape back a few more frames.

"What are you doing?" Sammy asked.

"Trying to see if I can get a look at the person who moved that chair," Joe replied, staring intently at the screen.

Joe ran the sequence through several times before finally admitting defeat. "It's no use, Sammy," Joe said glumly. "The lighting's not good enough, and there are too many people in the foreground to make a positive ID. About all I can tell from this tape is that whoever moved the chair is probably a man because of the size of the hands."

"Well, I know more than I knew before," Sammy offered. "I watched that tape four or five times and never noticed someone move that chair."

Joe frowned, tapping the notebook with his pencil. "You told me Mitch Mayflower hurt his knee where you took away his title. Can you tell me anything more about what happened then?"

"Well, let's see," Sammy said as he sank back into the swivel chair. "I'd been in the IWA for less than a year, and when Mitch Mayflower said he'd take me on, it seemed like my big break. Mitch was the champion, and I was the new kid on the block."

"Did Mitch have bad knees already?" Joe inquired.

"Yes, he did," said Sammy. "That was pretty common knowledge. Frankly, he shouldn't have been wrestling with such bad knees. Mitch was taking chances."

"And you think Missy believes you deliberately went after his knees to cripple him," said Joe.

Sammy nodded. "Definitely. See, before that match I was on friendly terms with both

Mitch and Missy. Since then, she bad-mouths me to the wrestling press every chance she gets. And she manages only bad-guy wrestlers, with the hope that one of them will take the title away from me. So far, she hasn't had any luck.''

"How did Mitch feel about you?" Joe inquired.

"When I went to see him in the hospital after the match, he told me not to blame myself," Sammy replied. "Mitch is a good guy. I don't think he holds a grudge."

Joe scribbled down a note, then asked Sammy, "Is there any other wrestler who might want to take you out, Sammy?"

Sammy shrugged. "It's possible. Maybe some guy's been using steroids and feels threatened by the campaign I began last year to keep steroids out of the IWA.

"Ever since Duke Dixon had a heart attack from using steroids last Christmas, I've been trying to convince Warfield to institute mandatory testing of all IWA wrestlers. He keeps saying he agrees with me one hundred percent, but he's still dragging his feet about mandatory testing. Maybe he's afraid he'll lose too many wrestlers."

"That's a possibility," Joe observed. "Who do you think uses them?"

"Major Disaster for one. I don't have any proof, but he bulked up awfully fast."

"Okay," Joe replied. "What about Tomahawk Smith?"

"I don't know," Sammy answered. "He's new to the IWA, and I don't know him well enough to say."

"How about your pal the Constrictor?"

"No way!" Sammy laughed. "Ethan would never use that garbage. He's too much of a health nut!"

"What about the Roman brothers?" Joe asked.

"It's possible. They're pretty pumped up, and I never see either of them do really serious weight lifting."

Joe put down his pencil. "Well, since Frank's tailing Disaster, I think I'll keep an eye on Missy. It's not much, but it's a start."

"Good," Sammy agreed. "I'll feel better if I know what she's up to."

"I hope she hasn't left." Joe went to the door and stuck his head out. Missy was standing with Warfield, the Constrictor, and a couple of guys from the camera crew, talking with them in a friendly, easy way.

Turning his head, Joe told Sammy, "I'm in luck! She's still here."

Joe watched then as Missy shook hands with Warfield and the Constrictor. Then she walked through the training center's main entrance.

"There she goes, Sammy. I'm going after her," Joe said in a low voice.

"Good hunting, pal," Sammy said as Joe slipped through the door.

Moving as quietly as possible, Joe trotted across the huge room after Missy. He paused at the entrance to make sure she wasn't in the lobby, but all he saw was a busload of tourists gawking at the photos of the IWA wrestlers on the wall. Joe moved forward to peer through the wide plate-glass windows at the front of the lobby and found Missy getting into a powder blue sedan.

When Joe stepped outside, Missy was already pulling out. Joe ran to his and Frank's black van and took off fast. He had to keep her in sight.

Missy turned right onto Tilghman Boulevard, the main thoroughfare that ran through Allentown. She traveled west on Tilghman, and Joe guessed she was heading for Bethlehem, the town right next to Allentown. Missy drove for about half an hour, seemingly unaware that she was being followed. Just before reaching Lehigh University, Missy made a quick left onto Fourth Street.

He followed her down Fourth until she turned into the front gates of a white two-story mansion. Joe looked up at the row of Greek columns in front of the house. Wow, this is some place, Joe thought to himself. His eyes traveled along the low stone wall surrounding the property and read the name Mayflower on a wrought-iron sign affixed to the wall.

Missy pulled her car in through the gates and parked in the circular driveway. She hopped out and hurried up the front steps.

Joe pulled up to the entrance and parked just in front of a gatekeeper's cottage. He still had a clear view of the front of the Mayflower mansion, including the driveway.

"Now at least I know where she lives," Joe said quietly to himself.

He watched the house, but absolutely nothing happened during the hour that the late-afternoon sun slowly dropped in the sky. Joe yawned as he began his second hour of surveillance.

He began to realize how tired he was from his workout with Frank and wished he could catch a quick nap. Before long his eyelids got heavy, and he drifted off to sleep.

It seemed as if his eyes had closed only for an instant when he felt a sharp jab on his shoulder.

Joe jerked awake to find himself looking down the two holes at the end of a double-barreled shotgun.

Chapter

4

FRANK'S ASSAILANT let him drop, and he fell flat on the ground. What's going on? Frank thought frantically to himself as he scrambled to his feet. He found himself face-to-face with Major Disaster.

"I saw you working out with the Kung Fu King at the gym today. Who are you, kid?"

"My name's Frank." Disaster grabbed Frank by the front of his shirt and lifted him until the two of them were nose to nose.

"Hey, take it easy! I'm a wrestler, too!" Frank cried out.

"What are you doing snooping around here?" asked Disaster.

"I'm one of your biggest fans, Major. I was working out with Sammy because he offered to show me the ropes. But I'd rather be a bad-guy wrestler like you. I've been wanting to meet you, so I followed you."

I hope he buys my story, Frank thought to himself.

"So can you put me down, please?" Frank pleaded, pretending to be more scared than he actually was.

Disaster held Frank out at arm's length for a moment, intently studying his face. Finally he let go of Frank.

"Thanks, Major," Frank said, brushing the dirt from his pants.

"I don't know if you're telling the truth or not, but you seem like too much of a kid to worry about."

"Hey, I'm a lot tougher than I look," Frank said defiantly. "I really thought if I could learn from you, I could make it as a pro wrestler. Can I at least talk to you?"

"No!" Disaster snarled. "Get out of here and don't follow me anymore! I might not be so gentle the next time I see you hanging around."

Frank turned away and walked around the corner of the building. He ducked into the doorway of a vacant storefront and gave Disaster a few minutes to go back inside. Then he made his way toward the parking lot. Frank saw that Disaster's car was still the only one in the lot.

Moving cautiously, Frank went around to the front of the office building, opened the double doors, and slipped inside.

He scanned the dimly lit lobby and saw that it was as shabby and dirty as the surrounding neighborhood.

"Must be the janitor's year off," Frank said as he took in the filthy floor, the graffiti on the walls, the dusty windows, and the overflowing ashtray beside the elevator doors.

Attached to the wall, just above the ashtray, Frank noticed the directory for the building, faintly illuminated by a twenty-five-watt bulb. Frank cast a quick glance around to see if anyone was approaching, but the building was as silent as a graveyard.

Frank hurried over to the directory and ran his finger down it. He saw that the tenants on the first floor were an accountant, a beauty salon, and a Jacob Walsh, M.D. He shot a quick glance down the hall and spotted the door to Dr. Walsh's office. The office was set along the outer wall of the ground floor, and Frank guessed that he had been outside one of Walsh's windows when he'd overheard the muffled shouting.

So the rear doorway Disaster had used probably opened right into Walsh's office, Frank thought. But why would he sneak in the back way? Unless he had a reason for not wanting to be seen.

Hearing voices raised down the hall, Frank turned and quickly left. He didn't want another run-in with the big wrestler. I'd better ask Sammy if he's ever heard of this Dr. Walsh, Frank decided. Maybe he knows of some connection between him and Major Disaster.

Once outside the building, Frank made a beeline to Sammy's car. He put the top down and sped off, grateful for the cool evening air that flowed over him.

Frank drove directly to Sammy's house. He aimed the automatic garage door opener at the small attached building and pulled the vintage sports car inside.

The door leading into the house from the garage was open, but Frank knocked before entering. Sammy called out a big hello from the kitchen counter, where he was eating a huge ham and cheese sandwich.

"How are you doing?" Sammy asked around a mouthful of sandwich. "Help yourself to some eats."

"Thanks. I will," Frank replied, moving to a cutting board on the kitchen counter piled high with sliced cheese and cold cuts. "Any word from Joe?"

"Nope," Sammy said, shaking his head. "Last I heard he was tailing Missy Mayflower."

"Leave it to Joe to follow the women!" said Frank, spreading mustard on a slice of rye bread.

"Did you learn anything?" Sammy wanted to know.

"Possibly. Have you ever heard of a Dr. Jacob Walsh?"

"I sure have, and none of what I've heard is good. He's got a bad reputation," Sammy answered, putting his sandwich down. "I'm pretty sure he supplies steroids to some guys in the IWA."

"Do you think Major Disaster uses them?" Frank asked as he piled ham and cheese on the bread.

"As I told Joe, it's possible," Sammy replied. "Disaster got an impressive physique in a big hurry. It's probably one of the reasons Missy Mayflower was able to make him into a star so fast."

"Speaking of Disaster, I ran into him outside of Walsh's office. Actually, he grabbed me while I was trying to look through one of Walsh's windows," Frank continued. He put his sandwich together for one big bite.

"Did he rough you up?" asked Sammy, concerned.

Frank shook his head as he chewed. "Not much. He recognized me from the gym, and I told him I was a big fan of his. I probably inflated his ego—if that's possible."

"Walsh and Disaster together . . . something stinks here," Sammy said. "I announced the other day that I'm going to make a public statement against steroid use before my match against Major Disaster on Saturday."

"So, you think maybe Walsh might be using Disaster to try to shut you up?" Frank speculated. "Maybe Walsh convinced Disaster that it was in his best interests to keep you quiet.

"Are there any other wrestlers besides Disaster who you think might use steroids?" he added.

"A few," Sammy replied. "But nobody knows how many because Stan Warfield keeps stalling about testing all the wrestlers in the IWA.

"If it could be proved that Disaster or any other wrestler was using steroids, he'd be kicked out of the IWA. Just like in any other professional sport, it's against IWA rules to use steroids."

Frank took another big bite of his sandwich as he quickly ran over what he'd learned about the case so far. He knew he had to find out what Joe had uncovered before he could decide what to do next.

"Well, if Disaster thinks you're trying to get him kicked out of the IWA, that could give him a strong motive to knock you out of wrestling. Say, Sammy, can I borrow your car again? I want to go buy a six-pack of soda," Frank added as he stood peering into the refrigerator.

"Sure," Sammy said with a wave of his hand. "I forgot I was out of soda."

"Stay on your toes until I get back, Sammy," Frank said after he finished his sandwich. "There's no telling when the next attack on you will come."

"Don't worry. I've got the best alarm system money can buy. Besides, Ethan's coming over to watch videos tonight and keep an eye on me."

As Frank walked into the garage, he passed through an electric eye that triggered the outer garage door. The door was rising as Frank slid into the sleek red sports car and fastened his seat belt.

Enjoying the soft comfort of the car's leather interior, Frank revved the powerful engine, threw it into reverse, and backed out into the street.

Suddenly the lights of a car parked nearby flicked on, and its engine roared to life.

Frank was still backing up when he realized that the car was accelerating and heading straight toward him.

Hey! Frank thought. Is that guy blind? He's going to broadside me!

Frank tried to push the gearshift into first, but the clutch stuck. Frantically he pushed on the stick, trying to put the car into a forward gear.

The mysterious sedan raced closer, and still the shift wouldn't move. Frank glanced out at the oncoming car. The light from its headlights moved forward and quickly filled the side window. Unable to see, Frank tensed for the crash that he knew was coming.

Chapter

5

"MIND TELLING ME what you're doing trailing my sister, kid?" the guy at the other end of the shotgun asked Joe.

"I wasn't—" Joe started to say, but the big man holding the double-barreled twelve-gauge cut him off. Hey, this guy is Miracle Mitch Mayflower, Joe thought to himself.

"Don't try to deny it. Missy saw you following her," Mitch said, pulling open the door on the driver's side of the van. "Come on." He motioned with the shotgun barrel. "You're coming into the house. I have to decide whether or not to call the cops."

"There's no need to do that," Joe said, flashing an embarrassed smile. "It's easy to explain."

"Explain inside," Mitch replied, and he backed off a few steps.

Joe stepped out of the van, conscious of the shotgun that was still leveled at his chest.

Joe walked slowly up the driveway, Mitch Mayflower at his side. From the corner of his eye Joe glanced at his captor. He noticed the man's pronounced limp, undoubtedly the result of his wrestling injury. Joe caught a dangerous gleam in Mitch's eyes when their gazes met briefly. This guy knows how to handle himself in any rough situation, Joe thought.

"Hey," Joe said, "aren't you Miracle Mitch Mayflower?"

The big man's hard expression broke, and his blue eyes widened in surprise. "Yeah! Are you a wrestling fan?"

"I'm not only a fan, I'm a wrestler, too," Joe replied.

"Oh, yeah?" Mitch said. "Well, then we ought to have a lot to talk about," he said good-naturedly, opening the front door of the house and backing inside. Although Mitch was acting sort of friendly, Joe noticed that the ex-wrestler still kept the shotgun trained on him.

Joe stepped through the doorway and found himself in a foyer with pearl gray walls, a black marble floor, and an ornate crystal chandelier overhead. Joe was very impressed.

"Over here." Mitch gestured toward a door just off the hall.

Joe pushed the door open to see Missy May-flower lounging on a huge black leather sofa. Her icy stare cut right through Joe and almost made him shudder.

Mitch motioned for Joe to sit down on a chair across from the couch. Then Mitch tapped Missy so she would scoot over to give him room to sit down. He sat next to his sister, laying the big gun across his knees.

"First things first," Mitch said. "What's your name?"

"Joe Hardy, Mr. Mayflower."

"Okay, Joe, why were you following Missy?" Mitch asked bluntly.

"I—" Joe pretended to stumble over his words. He lowered his head and tried to look embarrassed as he answered. "Well, it's like I started to tell you, Mr. Mayflower, that I want to be a professional wrestler. While I was working out at the IWA gym today, I saw Missy, and . . ." Joe's voice trailed off.

"So, you've got a crush on my little sister, huh?" Mitch chuckled.

Joe dropped his head. "Uh, yeah, Mr. Mayflower, I guess I do. I followed Missy to find out where she lived. I was sitting in my van, trying to get up enough nerve to come up to the front door to ask her out. I guess I fell asleep. I had a pretty tough workout at the gym today."

Joe raised his eyes to Missy and Mitch to

see if they were buying his story, and he was relieved to see that Missy looked a bit flattered. When he checked out Mitch, he saw the big man flick the safety catch on the shotgun, which he set on the glass and marble table before him. The big man's handsome face was creased with a broad grin.

"What do you think, Missy?" Mitch asked. "Should we introduce him to the old man?"

"No! I saw him at the gym today hanging around with that creep Sammy Rand. Any friend of—"

"Stop it, Missy! It wasn't Sammy's fault that I got hurt. You've got to stop blaming him for that," Mitch said sternly.

"I'm sorry, Mitch," Missy said, and lowered her head. After a moment she glanced up at Joe. "Do you know who our dad is, Mr. Hardy?"

"Sure. He's Mike 'the Maestro' Mayflower, the man who succeeded Gorgeous George as the superstar of wrestling," Joe said, grateful that he'd remembered the article he'd just read in a wrestling magazine.

"Okay, Mitch, perhaps Daddy should meet this guy," Missy said, her expression softening.

Before he knew it, Joe was being ushered into a room on the other side of the hall. It was filled with souvenirs and trophies from Mike Mayflower's professional wrestling career. Mike himself was sitting in a huge armchair reading the newspaper. On a television set in the corner, columns of stock-market quotations scrolled down the screen.

The first thing Joe noticed was the amazing resemblance between father and son. Mike was an older version of Mitch, with white hair and a few more wrinkles. Next Joe noticed the way the old man's chest and arm muscles bulged under what was obviously an expensive yellow cashmere sweater.

"What have we here, a visitor?" the older Mayflower asked in a gravelly voice.

"A would-be wrestler with eyes for Missy," answered Mitch.

"Is that a fact?" Mike rose to shake hands. "What's your name, son?"

"I'm Joe Hardy, Mr. Mayflower. It's a real honor to make your acquaintance."

"Can the mister, Joe. Call me Mike," the older wrestler said in a friendly voice.

"Thanks, Mike," Joe replied. "Meeting you and your son in the same day is a real treat. I've got videotapes of some of your matches from the fifties and sixties, against Gorgeous George, Man Mountain Dean, and the Swedish Angel."

"No kidding." Mike's eyes twinkled with pleasure. "I'm amazed any of those matches survived. Not that many of them were filmed, you know."

"The tapes I have were copied from old kinescopes, made before they had videotape," Joe explained, glad he had seen his friend Chet Morton's old wrestling videotapes.

"Boy, it's been years since I've seen some of that stuff. You'll have to tell me where you got those tapes," Mike said enthusiastically as he motioned for Joe to sit down. Joe saw Missy and Mitch seat themselves in chairs on either side of their father. Joe sat down on a chair across from them.

Joe glanced over at Missy. Although she appeared to be relaxed, she still looked suspicious.

Joe turned his attention back to Mike Mayflower. "If you'd like, Mike, I'd be happy to send you the video company's address."

"You would?" Mike's eyebrows shot up as he grinned. "That'd be great. Then I could show Mitch how I creamed Man Mountain Dean in fifty-two. Now, that was a great match.

"Hey, I know what," Mike suggested. "Let's have Joe to dinner tonight." The old man leaned forward and slapped Joe on the knee. "How about it, Joe? Have you eaten yet?"

"No," Joe replied, delighted not only at the prospect of digging deeper into the case, but also at getting to know Missy better.

"Missy, would you tell Clarice that we have one more for dinner?"

After a dinner of roast beef, baked potatoes, and double-chocolate cake for dessert, Mike Mayflower pushed away from the dinner table, patting his stomach in satisfaction. Then he looked over at Joe and said, "Come on. I'll take you on the five-cent tour of my little shack.

"Want to help me show Joe around the house, kids?" Mike asked.

"I'd like to, Dad, but I've got a date later," Mitch explained.

"Okay, have fun," Mike said with a smile. "How about you, Missy?"

"No, thanks, Dad. I have to make some phone calls about the Major's next match."

"Suit yourself," Mike replied. Then he turned to Joe and said, "Well, Joe, I guess it's just you and me."

Joe decided that this would be a good time to try to learn as much as he could about Missy and Disaster from Mike. But he knew he had to be careful not to get Mike suspicious.

Mike led Joe through the long dining room, past a wall of stained-glass windows, and into the next room. Every inch of wall space was covered with framed swords, pistols, knives, flintlocks, crossbows, and other weapons so obscure Joe didn't immediately recognize them.

45

"Wow," Joe said, impressed. "This is quite a collection."

"It's taken me twenty years to put it together," Mike said modestly. "It's one of the best private collections on the East Coast."

"I read that Major Disaster is a real military buff. I bet he's fascinated by all this stuff," Joe ventured.

The cheery expression left Mike's face at Joe's mention of Major Disaster. "The Major's never seen it. I won't have him in my house."

"Why is that? Your daughter *is* his manager."

"I don't like the guy. I'm sorry Missy ever got mixed up with a jailbird like him," Mike growled.

"A jailbird! What'd he do?"

"He used to be a leg breaker for a loan shark. He got into wrestling after he got out of prison."

"Exactly why is Missy managing Disaster?" Joe asked.

"She's determined to manage any wrestler who can take away Sammy Rand's title. Missy hates Sammy so much she doesn't care how she does it," Mike told him, an edge of anger creeping into his voice.

"Mitch doesn't blame Sammy for what happened to him," Joe pointed out. "Why does Missy?"

"I don't know, kid," Mike said with a bewildered expression. "It's an obsession with her."

Sensing it was time to change the subject, Joe asked Mike another question. "Say, Mike, were steroids a problem when you were wrestling?"

"Huh?" The old wrestler gave Joe a strange look. "Steroids? Nope. Wrestlers didn't use that stuff in my day. Why do you ask?"

"Sammy Rand thinks steroids are a major problem with the IWA. He's even trying to get Stanley Warfield to make testing for steroids mandatory."

"Yeah? Good for Sammy," Mike said approvingly. "I keep trying to convince Missy that Sammy's okay, but she just won't listen."

"How does Missy feel about steroids?" Joe inquired.

"She's against them," Mike replied firmly. "I know she felt pretty bad about that kid in the IWA who died from using steroids last month."

"Do you think Major Disaster uses steroids?"

"I don't know. But I'll tell you one thing—if he is using them and Missy finds out about it, she'll drop him like a hot potato."

Filing that bit of information away for future reference, Joe decided he'd better make his exit. He was eager to tell Frank about his eventful evening.

"I think it's time I go. Please say good night to Missy and Mitch for me," Joe said politely.

"Will do. Good night, Joe, I'm sure you can find your way out."

With those words Mike turned and walked down the hallway toward a wide staircase that led upstairs.

Boy, the Mayflowers are some family, Joe said to himself as he walked toward the front door. He passed a small side table beneath a gold-edged mirror and noticed Missy's purse, which had been carelessly tossed on top of the table. Its clasp was open. Casting a quick glance behind him, Joe stuck his hand into the purse and immediately touched something cold and hard wrapped loosely in a silk scarf. Puzzled, Joe withdrew the heavy object and whipped the scarf off it.

It was a bowie knife. As Joe scrutinized its sharp, wedge-shaped blade, he realized it was the perfect tool for sawing through a thick rope.

Chapter

6

WHAT'S GOING ON? Frank thought to himself as the sedan raced closer and closer. At the last possible instant before impact, Frank slammed his foot down on the gas pedal and spun the wheel hard, to the right. The car zoomed backward and swung out in a wide arc. The sedan zipped past.

Frank breathed a sigh of relief. He strained to check out the sedan, but it was moving too fast for him to identify. Besides, whoever was driving the car had put out the rear license plate light.

The first thing Frank wondered was if Disaster had trailed him from Walsh's office. Then, since he was driving Sammy's car, he wondered if the attack had been meant for Sammy. Whoever's responsible for those attacks on Sammy might have been behind that wheel, Frank thought to himself.

Frank was afraid to drive Sammy's car after it wouldn't go into gear. He managed to get it back to neutral and pushed it back into Sammy's garage.

"I thought you were going to the store," Sammy commented when Frank came in.

"I changed my mind. Your car wouldn't shift, and then somebody decided to play chicken with me as I was pulling out."

"What?" Sammy's eyes widened in surprise.

"Someone tried to broadside your car. They split before I could get a plate number or a make on the car."

"Man, what a day," Sammy said, shaking his head. "All these incidents are starting to get to me. I think I'll cancel with Ethan and just go to bed. Tell Joe I said good night."

"Okay, Sammy. Why don't you double-check the alarm system before you turn in. I'm going to do some background checks on the computer while I wait for Joe."

Frank sat down at the small desk in Sammy's guest bedroom, where he had set up his computer, modem, and fax machine. He quickly gained access to the national law enforcement data network his father, Fenton Hardy, used in his work as a private investigator.

First Frank keyed in Major Disaster's real

name, Fred J. Stone. Frank had a strong suspicion that Disaster had a criminal record—he was right, of course. Quickly scanning the screen, Frank noted multiple arrests for assault and illegal possession of firearms, and one for attempted murder! Bingo, Frank said to himself.

Next Frank requested a copy of Disaster's "rap sheet" to be faxed to him. Frank did have to admit to himself that a criminal record alone was no proof that Disaster was behind the mysterious attacks on Sammy.

Frank finished reviewing the rap sheet and next keyed in Missy Mayflower's name. Frank found no information on her in the national law enforcement data bank, so he tried the Allentown police computers next. Besides a few parking tickets, he saw that Missy had only been cited twice, both times for making harassing phone calls to Sammy Rand. A quick check of the dates showed that this had occurred immediately after the match with Mitch. In both cases the charges had been dropped. Frank called up a copy of Missy's record on the fax anyway.

Next Frank decided to check out some of the other wrestlers. He started with Tomahawk Smith, but Smith had no criminal record. Frank was about to check out another one when Joe walked in.

"Hi, Joe. How'd it go?"

"Well," Joe began as he seated himself across from Frank at the small table. "It started with Mitch Mayflower getting the drop on me with a twelve-gauge shotgun."

"What! How did that happen?"

Joe looked abashed. "I fell asleep while I was watching Missy's house."

Frank let out a sigh. "Whew! You were lucky you didn't get your head blown off."

"I talked my way out of it by pretending to be a novice wrestler with a crush on Missy. Mitch even took me in to meet his dad, Mike 'the Maestro' Mayflower."

"Hey, wasn't he an old-time wrestling star?" asked Frank.

"Yep," Joe replied. "So, anyway, after I had dinner with the Mayflowers, I talked with Mike and got some info on Missy and Major Disaster. Then on my way out I saw that Missy had left her purse lying on a table by the door, so I checked through it for any clues. Inside, I found a very sharp bowie knife that would have been perfect for slicing through a thick climbing rope."

"I found something else that doesn't look good for Missy," Frank announced, quickly filling Joe in on what he had learned about Missy's harassment of Sammy. "And it gets worse. Fred Stone, also known as Major Disaster, has a rap sheet as long as my arm."

"That coincides with what I learned from Mike Mayflower," Joe told his brother.

"I think Major Disaster and Missy might be trying to shut Sammy up permanently so he won't speak out against steroids," Frank said. "I ran into Disaster outside the offices of a Dr. Walsh, who Sammy thinks has been supplying steroids to some of the wrestlers."

"If Sammy's antisteroid campaign *is* the motivation for the attacks, then maybe we can cross Missy off our list of suspects. Mike told me that Missy is totally against the use of steroids," Joe pointed out.

"Well, maybe Disaster's working alone," Frank suggested. "Anyway, while you were gone, a car almost broadsided me while I was driving Sammy's car.

"I'm not sure if that means I was followed by Disaster, or if it was because I was driving Sammy's car, but either way we all have to be very careful.

"There's not much more we can do until morning," Frank told his brother, stifling a yawn. "Let's hit the sack so we can get an early start tomorrow."

The next morning, after a quick breakfast, the Hardys and Sammy set out for the garage and then the IWA training center. Frank rode with Sammy in his car, and Joe followed them to Sammy's mechanic's garage in case the car broke down on the way. After dropping off the car, they all piled into the van and drove to the IWA center.

When they entered the main gym of the center, Frank saw that there were already at least thirty wrestlers and trainers beginning their workouts. Among the group Sammy pointed out the Constrictor, Tomahawk Smith, Baron Von Krupp, and Major Disaster to him. Missy was nowhere to be seen.

In the center of the room and just beyond the three main practice rings, Frank noticed a pair of almost identical wrestlers working out on a mat. Several mats were laid out on the floor near them.

"Let's limber up over by those guys, Joe," Frank suggested.

"You guys go ahead," said Sammy. "I have to check in with Slim."

"Sure," Joe said, following Frank into the locker room. The Hardys set down their gym bags and changed into wrestling tights, knee pads, boots, and protective headgear.

"Ready to try a few falls, Frank?" Joe challenged as they walked over to the mats. "I bet I can pin you today without Sammy coaching you."

"I wouldn't be so sure of myself if I were you," Frank retorted.

"If you guys are looking for a match, how about trying something really challenging?"

Joe heard a slightly sarcastic voice from behind him.

He turned around to see the two nearly identical wrestlers standing at the edge of his mat.

"Both you guys look like you could use a serious workout," said the taller of the two men.

"We're tough enough to take on you two refugees from a Hercules picture," Joe snapped.

"Who are these guys, anyway?" Frank asked Joe.

But before Joe could reply, the shorter brother rolled his blue eyes disbelievingly and snapped, "We're the Romans, the hottest tag team in wrestling. My name's Victor, short for Victory, punk!"

"Yeah, and I'm Jimmy," his brother added. "Who are you guys?"

Joe turned to his brother with a look of disgust on his face. Then he turned back and focused on the opposition. "We're Frank and Joe Hardy. How do you want to do this?"

"In a tag-team match, of course," Victor answered with a sneer. "I'm sure you rookies can use the practice."

"That remains to be seen," Frank retorted.

"I'm going to enjoy teaching you two a lesson," Jimmy Roman said as he smacked a huge fist into the palm of his other hand.

"Follow us, rookies," Victor Roman said,

leading the Hardys to the ring in the center of the room.

When they were all assembled in the ring, Frank noticed that the other wrestlers and trainers had stopped their workouts and were clustered along the ropes that surrounded the ring.

"Now, you two know the rules of a tag-team match?" Jimmy Roman asked with a sneer.

"Sure," Joe replied. "Only one wrestler from each team in the ring at a time. The man in the ring can make a substitution only by touching his partner's hand. The untagged man has five seconds to get out of the ring."

"Very good," Victor Roman said sarcastically. "Little Joey has obviously done his homework."

"Easy, Joe," Frank warned as he passed him on the way out of the ring. "Don't let him rile you. It's just a trick to make you careless."

As soon as Jimmy left the ring, Frank saw Victor and Joe square off against each other.

"Now's the time to pull out your best moves," Victor taunted as they circled each other.

"Ha!" Joe retorted. "You think I'd waste my best moves on you?"

"That's the spirit, kid. Don't let the Romans buffalo you," the Constrictor shouted encouragingly.

"Tear his head off, Victor!" Major Disaster yelled. "If Kung Fu taught him to wrestle, it ought to be easy!"

Suddenly Victor charged forward and tried to grab Joe's head. Joe ducked under Victor's arms, pivoted, and shot his arms under Victor's in a double hammerlock.

Victor went down on one knee and whipped his upper body back and then forward, and Joe was tossed off.

Victor launched himself into the air, landing on Joe with a full body slam.

"Oooohh!" Joe grunted, his face contorted with pain. Using a quick kick, Joe threw Victor off. The Constrictor and a few other wrestlers cheered Joe's escape, while Disaster led Tomahawk Smith and the rest of the bad-guy wrestlers in booing Joe and cheering Victor. Victor rolled to his feet, dived into the ropes, and rebounded back into Joe.

Frank saw his brother sidestep Victor, catching him with a clothesline move across the throat. Victor dropped, and Joe hurled himself on top of the larger man.

"One, two—" Frank counted off, but his count was interrupted by the sight of Jimmy Roman hurling himself over the top rope and into the ring.

Jimmy hurled his entire weight onto Joe's

back, knocking Joe off Victor and onto the mat.

"Hey, you can't do that!" Frank shouted, and he, too, leapt into the ring.

Victor Roman met his charge with a knee to Frank's midsection, and Frank went down.

Then, while Frank gasped for breath on the mat, he saw the Romans grab Joe and hurl him into the ropes. Then Jimmy slammed Joe on the side of the head with a blow from his forearm.

Joe went down hard, and the Romans tossed him into the ropes again, twining the flexible ropes around his arms.

Frank desperately tried to get up, but Victor slammed him back down to the mat with a two-fisted ax-handle punch.

Before Frank could make any countering moves, he felt Victor pick him up around the waist and hold him upside down.

Hanging with his head down, he saw Jimmy Roman climb up to the top of the corner post. From Frank's position it looked as if Jimmy was getting ready to fly through the air. In a flash of realization that sent chills through his body, Frank knew he was being set up for a spiked pile driver, an illegal move that could break his neck!

Chapter

7

JOE TRIED TO FREE HIMSELF from the ropes, but they held fast. In a minute Jimmy Roman would deliver the spiked pile driver move against Frank's feet that would drive his head into the mat and snap his neck!

Joe stopped straining against the ropes for a moment and tried rotating his arms to loosen the ropes. He worked fast, knowing that his brother's life was at stake.

"Hey, you guys are going too far!" shouted the Constrictor. Joe's hopes rose as he realized Sammy's friend was coming to Frank's aid.

Suddenly Major Disaster planted himself in the Constrictor's path. "Not so fast, pal. I think we ought to let them finish their match,"

Disaster said, placing a beefy hand on the Constrictor's chest.

"Get out of my way, Major!" the Constrictor said, slapping Disaster's hand away. "The Romans will kill that kid!"

"Let them!" Disaster snarled, grabbing Constrictor's arm and twisting it behind his back.

"You're way out of line, Major!" Tomahawk Smith shouted as he ran over to the two struggling wrestlers. Joe saw that the Romans had been momentarily distracted by the confrontation outside the ring.

Finally Joe pulled free from the ropes and charged Jimmy Roman.

"Yaaaaaa!" Joe shouted as he plowed into Jimmy, the force of his attack throwing Jimmy off the post and out of the ring.

Victor Roman dropped Frank on his head and rushed to his brother's aid. Luckily, Frank wasn't hurt. He sprang up a second after he hit, then launched himself at Victor, who was just stepping through the ropes.

"If you're so fond of tying people in the ropes, let's see how you like it!" Frank shouted, twining the top and middle ropes around Victor's left arm.

While Frank was occupied with Victor, Joe had gotten out of the ring and was grappling with Jimmy Roman. Joe rolled between Jimmy's wide-spread legs, snagged Jimmy's ankle, and whipped it backward. The hulking wrestler tumbled forward on his face.

Joe instantly leapt on Jimmy, wrapping his arms and legs around Jimmy's spread-eagled arms, with the back of one arm pressing mercilessly against the back of Jimmy's neck.

"What's going on out here?" Sammy shouted angrily from across the gym.

Joe looked over to see Sammy standing outside his dressing room dressed in black sweatpants and a black tank top.

"It's just a friendly little practice bout," Victor Roman grunted from where he strained to free himself.

"Well, it doesn't look friendly to me!" Sammy said angrily as he stalked over to the ring.

"You got that right, Sammy!" the Constrictor said from where he was being held back from Disaster by a couple of trainers. "The Romans were warming up to do a spiked pile driver on your buddy here."

"Oh, yeah?" Sammy said. "If I ever see you Romans try that move again, I'll make double sure you're both kicked out of the IWA! You got me?"

"Yeah, we heard you," Jimmy said sullenly.

"Kung Fu, you wimp! Let them fight! They had a good bout going till you butted in!" Joe heard Major Disaster shout. "Why don't you stop being such a Goody Two-Shoes and mind your own business?"

"Why don't you butt out instead, Disaster? As long as I'm champ, I have an obligation to all the wrestlers in the IWA to make sure nobody gets hurt. I don't want anyone using the spiked pile driver even in a practice bout!" Sammy said, sauntering over to Disaster, his fists lightly clenched.

"In a pig's eye!" Disaster spat out. "You're so high and mighty. You think you can boss everybody in the IWA around, don't you?"

Disaster shoved Sammy in the chest with both hands. Instantly the two men were at each other. Tomahawk Smith and the Constrictor jumped in and tried to keep the two wrestlers apart while the Romans stood back, laughing at the confrontation.

"All right! Take it easy!" Joe shouted, making a grab at Disaster.

Frank pushed between Sammy and Disaster while Tomahawk and Constrictor held them back. "Come on, Sammy, be smart. Don't let him antagonize you," Frank said in a calm voice. "Remember what you always told us about mastering your anger."

"Don't listen to these punks, Sammy! Let's get it on! Right here!" Disaster shouted.

"We won't solve anything here," Sammy admitted. "But I'll see you in the ring Saturday, Disaster, and we'll see who comes out on top then.''

"It'll be me!" Disaster sneered. "Better polish up the IWA trophy belt, Sammy. I like it nice and shiny.''

Disaster turned and straight-armed Frank out of the way as he sauntered back toward the locker room.

"Come on, guys. Let's practice at the other end of the gym until the air clears. It stinks in here,'' said Sammy.

Sammy led the Hardys and the Constrictor to workout mats spread out at the far end of the gym.

While Frank and Joe watched, Sammy and the Constrictor practiced their moves. "Guys like Disaster and the Romans make me wonder what I'm doing in this business,'' Sammy said, disgusted.

"Take those punks the Romans," the Constrictor said as he rose from the mat. "They come off like they're so tough, but the truth is, they're losers.''

"Really?" Joe remarked.

"Yeah,'' the Constrictor went on. "They couldn't make it in the NAAW, so now they're giving the IWA a shot. You see, Victor's got a glass jaw. One tap and he's out like a light.''

"I guess that explains why he has to prove he's so tough,'' Frank observed.

"Uh, Sammy," Joe started. "When you have a free minute, Frank and I would like to talk with you."

"Don't worry," Sammy said, shooting a look at the Constrictor. "Ethan knows that you guys are here to investigate the little accidents I've been having."

"Well, in that case," Joe announced, "I forgot to tell you I found out something very interesting last night during my visit to the Mayflower mansion. As I was leaving, I found a bowie knife in Missy's purse."

"A bowie knife, huh? That could have cut through the climbing rope," Sammy said with a troubled expression.

"Like butter," Joe elaborated. "I know Frank told you about following Disaster to Dr. Walsh's office. It's starting to look like Disaster and Missy are double-teaming you. Disaster's trying to keep you from making that antisteroid speech before your match with him in two days, and Missy's out to get you because she blames you for Mitch's injury."

"Let them try," Sammy said grimly. "Nothing will stop me. I'm going to make that speech no matter what!"

"That's the spirit!" Joe cheered. "If Missy and Disaster are after you, we'll triple-team them—you, me, and Frank!"

"Hey, don't forget me," the Constrictor added.

"How could anyone forget you, Ethan." Sammy grinned, his expression lightening. "In the meantime, there's just one obstacle between me and my Saturday match with Disaster—a six-foot-six newcomer named Tomahawk Smith.

"I've got to be in top shape to wrestle him, because I've seen this kid wrestle and he's good. He's fast and he's got tremendous upper body strength."

"Then let's get to work," the Constrictor said, taking a wrestling stance in the middle of the mat.

After a grueling wrestling workout with the Constrictor, followed by squats, bench presses, and curls with free weights, Sammy said his morning workout was finished.

"Listen, guys. I'm going to hit the sauna for a while. I want to be sure I'm not over my weight limit for my bout."

"Sammy, if I ate like you do, I'd be worried about my weight, too," Joe shot back.

Pretending to get angry, Sammy threw a towel at Joe on his way out of the weight room. "Thanks a lot, Joe," Sammy said sarcastically.

"I'm not up for a sauna, but how about a shower, Joe?" Frank suggested after Sammy was gone. "I feel pretty grimy."

As they crossed the training center's main

room, Joe automatically kept an eye out for Major Disaster and the Romans. Although the huge room was full of wrestlers and trainers, there was no sign of Disaster or the Romans.

Joe followed Frank into the locker room, where they removed their headgear and began unlacing their wrestling boots.

As he was loosening his second boot, Frank heard the locker room door creak open and an angry voice drifted in.

"Man, if there hadn't been so many people around, I'd have kicked Sammy's teeth in for talking to us like that!"

"Keep your voice down, Vic! No point in getting so worked up right now," Joe heard Jimmy Roman reply. "He'll get his. And after Sammy's been dealt with, we'll settle accounts with those two punks. I think the blond one loosened one of my teeth."

"I can't wait to see that creep Sammy get what he deserves," Victor said nastily.

"His time will come, but in the meantime, keep your trap shut, Vic. Your big mouth could blow everything."

Putting a finger to his lips to indicate that they should be silent, Frank led Joe toward the locker room door.

Once they were out in the gym, Joe put his head close to Frank's and whispered, "Do you want to tell Sammy what they just said?"

"Absolutely!" Frank whispered back as he

turned and trotted off toward the steam room. Joe followed him into the hallway that led to the examination rooms, the doctor's office, the hydrotherapy room, and the steam room.

The steam room was deserted when they entered. Joe looked around for the sauna doors, and his heart skipped a beat when he saw them. Looped around the double door handles was a thick steel chain and a padlock.

"Sammy's been locked in!" Joe shouted, tearing over to the door. A moment fumbling with the chain showed him that it couldn't be broken without tools.

Both Joe and Frank tugged on the double doors and succeeded in opening them a crack.

They immediately had to retreat from the intense heat that poured through the crack. Frank checked the thermometer beside the door.

"Joe, it's a hundred and fifty degrees in there! We've got to get Sammy out before he's roasted alive!"

Joe peered through the glass window. "It may already be too late!" he cried as he spotted Sammy's flushed, sweaty form lying face-down on the floor of the sauna.

Chapter

8

JOE POUNDED HIS FIST on the door to the steam room.

"This'll let some of the heat out. Stand back—we're in for a real hot blast." Frank smashed the sauna windows with a metal bucket he found on the floor. Frank and Joe stepped back as intense heat poured out.

Frank checked the thermometer and saw that the mercury was slowly rising. It almost read one hundred and sixty degrees now!

"The thermostat controls must be inside the sauna," Frank observed.

"We've got to get inside fast then!" Joe shouted. He yanked on the doors again.

"Get help! Go find anybody to get these doors open," Frank said, still studying the chained doors. He heard the door slam shut behind him as Joe left the room.

Suddenly Frank's expression brightened. "I've got it! I'll pry the pins out of the hinges!"

Frank ran his eyes over the room looking for anything he could use to pry up the hinges. Sammy's gym bag, which sat on a redwood bench beside the sauna doors, caught his attention. He dumped the contents on the bench and quickly pawed through Sammy's soap, toothbrush, razor, and shaving cream.

"Aha!" Frank shouted triumphantly, holding up a metal comb and a hairbrush.

"It isn't much, but I think it'll work!" Frank said, and squatted next to the bottom hinge of the left door. He carefully slipped the teeth of the comb into the narrow space between the top of the pivot pin and the barrel of the hinge. He wiggled the teeth up and down, drawing the pivot pin up until he had enough room to jam one end of the comb under the rim of the pin. Using the metal comb like a wedge, Frank hammered the other end with the back of the hairbrush until he'd knocked the pin out of the top of the barrel.

Frank popped the pin out of the top hinge, too, and then tried to pull the door open, but it was too heavy.

Frustrated, he slammed his fist into the double doors. Luckily, at that moment, the doors to the sauna room swung open, and Joe charged through with the Constrictor and Tomahawk Smith close behind. They pulled on the door until there was a space large enough for Frank to squeeze into the sauna.

"I'll get some cold water and towels!" Joe ran to the shower on the far side of the room.

"I'll get the doctor," Tomahawk Smith said over his shoulder on his way out the door.

"I'll go get Sammy!" Frank shouted as he let a blast of burning hot air escape before he squirmed through the narrow entrance. "Wait here, Ethan, and I'll hand Sammy out to you."

Frank didn't bother turning down the temperature control. He just raced inside the sauna, grabbed Sammy, and dragged him toward the door. Frank strained hard, sweat pouring off him as he pulled Sammy's body to the door. The Constrictor reached in and yanked Sammy through the opening.

"It's like an inferno in there!" Frank said, wiping the sweat out of his eyes. The Constrictor laid the unconscious Sammy on the cool tile floor.

Constrictor and Frank could do nothing until Joe got there except try to remember their basic first aid. Joe arrived with cold wet towels very quickly, and Frank laid them across Sammy's forehead, around his neck, and across his chest.

Then, while Joe went into the sauna to turn off the heat, Frank knelt next to Sammy and bathed his head and limbs with the cold water Joe had brought in a bucket.

In minutes Tomahawk Smith burst into the room, followed by a young black man in a suit who was carrying a medical bag. "I'm Dr. Towner," the man with the bag announced as he knelt beside Sammy. "What happened?"

"He was locked in the sauna with the heat turned up all the way. We don't know for how long," replied Frank.

"I'll need some ice," the doctor said to Tomahawk over his shoulder. "There's a machine down the hall."

The young doctor lifted one of Sammy's eyelids and peered into his eye. "I'll think he'll be okay," the doctor announced. "You did the right thing by cooling him down. Another few minutes and he could've suffered brain damage."

Moments later Tomahawk returned with a bucket filled with ice.

Frank watched as the doctor made compresses with the ice and wet towels and packed them tightly around Sammy's neck and the back of his head. Frank realized that Sammy was in good hands and turned his attention to the sauna.

"I can't shut it off, Frank," Joe said as he

emerged from the sauna red-faced and dripping wet.

"I'll get one of the maintenance guys to trip the circuit breaker for the sauna," the Constrictor volunteered.

"How's Sammy?" Frank asked Dr. Towner.

"His temperature's down, and he's starting to breathe normally. I think he'll be okay," Dr. Towner answered cautiously.

A moment later the Constrictor stuck his head through the sauna room doors and gave the Hardys a thumbs-up sign. "Sauna's off, guys."

"Great, thanks, Ethan," Frank told him.

"Let's see what's wrong with it, Frank," Joe suggested eagerly.

"Hold on," Frank replied. "Let's wait for it to cool down."

Frank waited a few more minutes before he led Joe into the still hot, but now bearable, sauna.

Frank immediately went over to the control panel to check for what temperature Sammy had set on the thermostat. He was surprised to see it set at only ninety degrees. When Frank touched the control knob, it felt wobbly.

"I think the thermostat's been tampered with."

"Can you get the cover panel off?" Joe asked, crowding closer behind his brother.

"I can try." Frank dug his fingernails under the edge of the cover. It pulled right out.

When Frank studied the thermostat mechanism, he saw that it had indeed been tampered with. Someone had jammed the thermostat in the maximum On position. Then the metal post that the control knob was attached to had been broken off.

"Looks like it was ripped out of the wall, then just shoved back in the hole," Frank observed, handing the panel to Joe.

"It's been tampered with, all right," Joe said, looking into the space containing the thermostat mechanism. "The control's been jammed all the way on!"

"Whoever did this had to know Sammy was heading for the sauna," Frank pointed out.

"Disaster and the Romans were in the training center before Sammy went into the sauna. It could have been one of them," Joe speculated.

"They're strong suspects, but we don't have any hard evidence to prove they're involved. We still have lots of investigating to do before we find out who's trying to kill Sammy," said Frank.

"Hey, speaking of Sammy," Joe said, "let's see how he is."

When they emerged from the sauna, they were relieved to see Sammy sitting up, supported by Dr. Towner. Tomahawk Smith had left, but the Constrictor was still standing near the door, watching Sammy with a relieved smile on his face.

"How are you doing, Sammy?" asked Joe.

Sammy smiled weakly. "I'm alive, thanks to you guys."

"If you're feeling better, I'd like to take you to a hospital to be examined," the doctor told Sammy.

"I'm fine, Doc, really," Sammy assured him.

"I don't agree, Sammy. You could have died in there. You're weak and dehydrated," the doctor said.

"You'd better listen to the man, Sammy," the Constrictor mumbled.

"But, Ethan," Sammy interrupted, "you know I've got two important bouts in the next two days. Plus, I have to work on my speech against steroid use. I can't afford to go to the hospital right now."

The young doctor shrugged and closed his medical bag. "All right," he said, sounding resigned. "It's your funeral. But I won't be held responsible for a patient who ignores my advice."

"Don't worry about Sammy, Dr. Towner," Joe put in. "Frank and I will take care of him."

"Make sure he gets plenty of rest and

drinks a lot of water," the doctor instructed before leaving.

"I see you're in good hands, so I guess I'll go finish my workout," the Constrictor said. He started to follow the doctor out.

"Oh," Sammy said quietly, "Slim's at the dry cleaner's picking up my costumes. When he gets back, let him know what happened."

"Will do, buddy," the Constrictor said over his shoulder as the door closed.

"Sammy, if you won't go to a hospital, at least let us drive you home," Frank suggested.

"Okay. I just hate hospitals—they give me the creeps," Sammy replied. "But I do feel pretty shaky. It probably would be a good idea to get some rest at home."

Frank dropped Joe off at the garage to pick up Sammy's car on the way to Sammy's house.

"Are you sure you feel good enough to wrestle Tomahawk Smith tomorrow, Sammy?" Frank asked, concerned.

"I have to, Frank. Don't you see, if I have enemies because I'm against steroids, they'll think they've stopped me if I don't wrestle Tomahawk Smith tomorrow or if I don't make my speech before the bout with Disaster on Saturday. I can't allow anyone to stop me!" Sammy declared.

"We're with you Sammy," Frank said.

"Joe and I will do everything we can to protect you and find out who's behind all these 'accidents.' "

They drove in silence the rest of the way to Sammy's house.

"Sammy, do you mind if I raid your refrigerator?" Joe asked as soon as he got back to Sammy's.

"Go ahead," Sammy said. "Get some stuff out for all of us. I'm feeling a little hungry myself."

Frank smiled to himself. That sounded more like the Sammy he knew.

"Sammy, do you remember who was around the sauna before you went in?" Joe asked as he popped a frozen pizza into the microwave.

Sammy scratched his head thoughtfully. "Yeah, I bumped into Major Disaster and Missy in the hall outside."

"Where was Missy? I didn't see her in the gym today," said Joe.

Sammy shrugged. "I think she was meeting with Warfield or something. Anyway, I had words with both of them, and Disaster promised to stomp my tail during Saturday's bout. I told him to give it his best shot, and then I went into the sauna."

"Was anyone else arou—" Frank began.

"Yeah," Sammy replied quickly. "I ran into Victor Roman coming out of the room.

He was in such a hurry he almost knocked me down."

At the mention of Victor Roman's name, Frank and Joe exchanged looks.

"Did he seem jumpy?" Joe asked.

"Uh-huh," Sammy answered. "But I just thought he was uncomfortable about bumping into me." Suddenly Sammy snapped his fingers as if remembering something. "Excuse me a minute, guys. I'd better check my phone messages before I forget."

Frank followed Sammy out of the kitchen and into the living room. He was relieved to see that Sammy's mood had begun to lighten a bit.

Sammy began to relax as he listened to a few messages from friends, along with a reminder from his agent about a television interview he was scheduled to do after the bout with Major Disaster. Sammy froze, though, as the next message began to play.

The gravelly voice on the tape was unfamiliar to Frank, but the menacing message was all too familiar. "Sammy Rand, you'd better not deliver that antisteroid speech you're planning. If you do, you'll wish you'd never been born!"

Chapter

9

THE ANSWERING MACHINE clicked off just as Joe entered with the pizza. He immediately noticed the worried look on Sammy's face.

"What happened?" Joe asked.

"There's a threat against me on my answering machine," Sammy told him.

"Who has your number?" Joe asked, setting down the tray of food.

"Even though my number's unlisted, my agent's got it, and Slim, and Sue, my girlfriend. She's in Europe right now. They have it at IWA headquarters, too," Sammy replied.

"Almost anybody in the IWA would have access to it, then," said Frank.

"Let's play back the message and see if we can get a clue as to who it is," suggested Joe.

"Good idea," Frank agreed. He turned to Sammy.

"Do you have a noise reduction system built into your stereo system?" asked Frank.

"Sure do," Sammy replied.

"Good, I want to play with the sound levels on the tape to see if there are any clues in the background noises." Frank popped the incoming-message cassette out of the answering machine.

Then he walked over to the stereo system and slipped the tape into the cassette deck. After it played out, Frank rewound the tape and adjusted the levels on the graphic equalizer.

The message played through several times, with Frank making various adjustments. But no one could pick up anything from the background noises.

"I'm stumped," Joe admitted. "There's nothing on that tape that gives us any idea where that call was made from."

"You're right," Frank said in a discouraged tone. "Do you recognize the voice?"

Sammy shook his head. "My guess is that whoever made the call was disguising his voice."

"With all these threats, Sammy, I think you should try to get Warfield to take them seriously. Make him listen to you!" said Joe.

"Joe's right," Frank agreed. "And if Warfield won't help, then maybe you have to go to the police."

Sammy sat down on the couch and thought for a few moments, pursing his lips. When he looked up at the Hardys, he spoke simply and with great resolve. "I'm still going to make that speech Saturday night, no matter what threats are made."

Frank exchanged a quick look with his brother and slowly shook his head. He knew that Sammy was determined to make his speech, and he also knew Sammy's attacker was just as determined that he wouldn't make it. Frank and Joe had to work quickly to find out who was behind all the attacks on Sammy. The next one might just succeed.

"Sammy, you stay here where you're safe and rest up," Joe said, breaking the silence. "Call Slim or Ethan and get him to come over and keep an eye on you. Frank and I are going over to the IWA office to talk to Warfield about what's been happening. We'll see if we can get the IWA to back you."

Fifteen minutes later Joe and Frank were trying to talk their way into Warfield's office. From the look on the face of Warfield's sour, middle-aged secretary, it was going to be an uphill battle, Joe judged.

"Ma'am, we've got to see Mr. Warfield.

I've already told you it's urgent!" Frank was saying.

"And I've already told you that you can't get in to see Mr. Warfield without an appointment. He's a very busy man," she replied with a glare.

Just then Warfield's door flew open.

"Mrs. Briggs, I need—"

"Mr. Warfield, we need to speak with you! It's an emergency!" Joe jumped in.

Warfield looked at the Hardys as if noticing them for the first time. "I've seen you two around the gym. Who are you kids?" he asked.

"We're Frank and Joe Hardy," Frank explained. "We're, uh, protégés of Sammy Rand, and we're very concerned about the recent attempts on his life."

"You mean all the accidents Sammy's been staging?" Warfield asked sarcastically.

"This isn't a joking matter, Mr. Warfield," Joe said. "Sammy's life is at stake."

"Okay," he said with resignation, "why don't you step into my office and tell me about it.

"Hold my calls for a few minutes, Mrs. Briggs," Warfield told his secretary as he stepped aside to let Frank and Joe enter before him.

The Hardys sat down on two chairs that faced Warfield's big wooden desk. Frank checked out the office, its walls covered with wrestling posters and framed pictures of various wrestlers.

Warfield sat down behind his desk. "Is this about the thing with the chair and the ammonia in the water bottle?"

"It's more than that now, Mr. Warfield," Joe cut in. "Since then there have been several more attempts on Sammy's life, as you well know. What about the climbing rope that got cut?"

"Or about the attempt to roast Sammy in the sauna?" Frank added.

"Of course I heard about the rope, but he could have cut that himself. My maintenance chief told me about the sauna, but I figured it was just a publicity stunt."

"A publicity stunt!" Joe shouted. "Sammy could have died in that sauna!"

"And if that's true, Mr. Warfield," Frank asked sarcastically, "do you mind telling me how Sammy chained the sauna doors from the outside?"

"Now, w-wait a minute, boys," Warfield sputtered. "I don't know how well you know Sammy, but he's a complete publicity hound. Publicity is the main reason for his antisteroid kick. He's trying to milk it for personal publicity because steroids are in the news now. Next month it'll be something else."

"Haven't you listened to a word we've

said?'' Joe asked. Despite his frustration at Warfield's stubbornness, he tried to keep the anger from creeping into his voice. "Just a little while ago somebody left a message on Sammy's answering machine that threatened him if he went ahead with his speech."

Warfield dismissed that with a wave of his hand. "So what? Wrestlers are always looking for ways to drum up publicity. A threat on a wrestler is always good for a few lines in the evening paper or a mention on the TV news. The fans eat this stuff up, boys."

"Does this mean you're not going to do anything about the attempts on Sammy's life?" Frank demanded.

"I don't believe that Sammy's in serious danger," Warfield said smugly. "If you can give me some real proof that his life is being threatened, then I'll have the IWA investigate. Until then, don't waste my time. I've really got better things to do, like promoting wrestling through legitimate channels."

With that, Warfield stood up and showed the Hardys out. Frank and Joe reluctantly left his office.

"That was a waste of time," Joe said, feeling angry at the way Warfield had dismissed them.

"I can't understand it," Frank commented. "It's almost as if Warfield wanted something to happen to Sammy."

"I'll say. He sure didn't seem too concerned about the welfare of the man who's the IWA's biggest drawing card," Frank said as they walked down the hall toward the lobby.

"He seemed to believe that everything that's happened to Sammy is just for publicity," Joe pointed out. He stopped walking as a sudden thought struck him.

"Okay, Joe, I know that look. What are you thinking?"

Joe paused for a moment before answering.

"It just hit me—Warfield seems so unconcerned about Sammy's safety, yet he's very concerned about publicity. Could it be possible that Warfield's behind these assaults on Sammy? Maybe he's doing it to hype interest in Sammy's next matches."

"If that's true, then there might be some people in the IWA who have similar stories about Warfield," Frank pointed out. "Let's go back to Sammy's place and check out that idea with him."

Joe agreed, knowing now that they would get little help from Warfield or the IWA in protecting Sammy.

The next morning was bright and hot, and Joe and Frank rose early. Over a quick breakfast of pancakes and eggs, the duo discussed the next stage of the investigation. Sammy had been asleep when they got back the day before, and they hadn't wanted to disturb him.

"What do you think about the possibility of Warfield being behind your accidents? He seems pretty bent on the publicity angle. Do you think he could be doing this to you to drum up publicity for the IWA?" asked Frank.

"I never thought of Warfield as a suspect," Sammy said, "but what you're saying does make sense. I guess we should keep our eyes on him."

"That's a good idea, Sammy. I also think Frank and I should go back to Walsh's office to see if we can establish a solid connection between him and Disaster," Joe suggested. "After that message on your phone machine, I feel Walsh and Disaster could be up to something."

"You may be right, Joe," Sammy agreed. "Put those two sleazebags together, and they're capable of anything. Go, check them out with my blessings."

"We'll catch up with you later at the training center," said Frank.

"Okay. Good luck, guys. And be careful."

An hour later Frank directed Joe to turn into the parking lot next to Walsh's office.

"Are you sure this is the right place?" Joe asked skeptically, studying the building and the surrounding neighborhood with obvious distaste.

"Yep. Here's the plan," Frank said as they climbed out of the van. "We'll say we're novice wrestlers who want to see Walsh. Then, if we can get in to see him—"

"We'll try to get some proof that he's supplying steroids," Joe finished excitedly.

"You got it," Frank agreed as they entered the run-down office building. "If we can get Walsh for supplying steroids, then maybe we can tie him to Disaster and the attacks on Sammy."

They passed through the building's dingy lobby and down the narrow hallway that led to Walsh's office. Joe opened the door to Dr. Walsh's office and stepped through the doorway into a small reception room.

Joe noticed a small receptionist's window in the corner and went over to it, with Frank following.

"Hi! We're here to see Dr. Walsh," Joe said brightly to the young nurse with bleached-blond hair.

She gazed back at Joe suspiciously. "Do you have an appointment?" she asked coldly.

"Uh, no, we don't," Joe replied. "But we're from the IWA, and, uh, some of the other wrestlers said that Walsh is the man to see."

"What, precisely, is wrong?" the nurse

asked. Joe noticed that she seemed to perk up at the mention of the IWA.

"We're feeling kind of run-down, miss," Frank interjected. "We thought maybe Dr. Walsh could give us some kind of tonic or vitamins to pick us up."

The young nurse looked doubtful. "Well, he doesn't usually see new patients without an appointment—"

"But we're wrestlers," Joe insisted. "I thought Dr. Walsh specialized in wrestlers."

The nurse looked a little uncertain. "I guess it'll be okay. Why don't you go into the examining room and wait for the doctor."

The nurse led Frank and Joe down a dingy hallway to the examining room.

"Well, what do you think?" Frank asked as soon as they were alone. "Should we do a little snooping?"

"I'm right behind you," replied Joe.

Frank walked across the black- and white-tiled floor to a set of cabinets.

Just as Frank suspected, they were locked. "This won't stop me," Frank said as he pulled a lock pick from his wallet.

Frank pulled the first cabinet open, and he and Joe began to examine the boxes of prescription medicines and various medical implements.

"Find any steroids?" asked Frank.

Joe glanced over at the garbage can and got an idea. "I'll check in here, Frank." Joe lifted the lid and carefully began to go through its contents. After a moment he spotted a small white box labeled Anabolic Steroids and grabbed it.

"Frank, I've got it," he said excitedly.

Suddenly Joe froze as he heard a man's voice loudly demanding to see Walsh immediately. He shoved the steroid box into his pocket.

"I'm sorry, Mr. Stone, Dr. Walsh isn't in right now, but if you could have a seat . . ." Joe heard the young nurse say in a flustered voice.

"And I think you're lying, little lady! I think that sleazy pill pusher's hiding in his office, 'cause I heard you talking to someone as I came in."

Joe heard footsteps rapidly approaching their door. He quickly scanned the small room for another way out, but there was only one door into the room.

Joe and Frank turned to the door just as it flew open. There stood Major Disaster, his huge form filling the doorway. When his gaze fell on Frank, his ugly face turned red with rage.

"I told you I'd take care of you if I saw you here again," Disaster said as he stepped toward Frank, wearing a deadly expression.

Chapter

10

"THIS IS THE SECOND TIME I've caught you here, kid!" Disaster snarled at Frank. "Didn't I tell you not to come back?" Disaster took a step closer to Frank.

"Hey, wait a minute! I can explain, Major!" Frank replied quickly.

"Yeah, what's your story this time?" Disaster took a step closer to Frank.

"You see, Major, I wasn't exactly truthful when you found me outside the office before." Frank tried to look sincere. He shot a look at Joe to make sure he'd play along. Joe met his eye and gave a slight nod.

"Yeah, I thought you were giving me the runaround," Disaster growled.

"The fact is, I wasn't feeling too well, and I thought Dr. Walsh could—"

The rest of Frank's words were drowned out by the arrival of Dr. Walsh.

"What's the meaning of this ruckus in my office?" Walsh shouted as he barged into the small examining room.

Frank took Walsh's appearance in at a glance. Walsh was a pot-bellied, round-shouldered man with thinning blond hair and a wispy blond mustache on his upper lip. He wore black-rimmed glasses with thick lenses. Behind his thick lenses, his pale blue eyes were small and beady. Frank disliked him immediately.

"It's easy to explain, Doctor," Joe said quickly. "My brother and I were waiting here to see you, when this guy came in and accosted us."

"You're not patients of mine," Walsh snapped. He peered at them suspiciously through his thick glasses. "What are you doing here?"

"Uh, well, the fact is, Doctor," Frank said, pretending to fumble with his words as he improvised his story, "Joe and I came to you on the advice of the Roman brothers."

"You see, we're wrestlers, Doc," Joe interjected. "The Romans said if we wanted to get bulked up quick, you were the man to see."

Frank saw Walsh's small eyes narrow even further. "I don't know what you're talking about. If you want to see me, you call me and make an appointment.''

Frank acted disappointed. "Gee, Dr. Walsh, we were sort of hoping we could see you today before we went back to our training.''

"You heard the man, make an appointment,'' Disaster growled in a low voice. "Now get out!''

Not wanting to anger Disaster any more, Frank and Joe left the examining room.

As they made an appointment with Walsh's nurse, Frank heard Disaster shouting angrily, "I'm a two-time loser, Doc. If they catch me doing what you've asked me to do, I might get into deep, deep trouble!'' Walsh's reply was inaudible. The Hardys exchanged looks, and then left the office.

"Should we tell Sammy what we found at Walsh's office?'' Joe asked when they reached the lobby.

"I want to do a little more snooping first,'' Frank said in a low voice. "Come on.'' He led Joe out of the building and cautiously went around to the rear of the building, where he spied a rusting Dumpster.

"Keep an eye out for Walsh and Disaster.'' Frank climbed up and leaned into the Dumpster, where he began sorting through its contents.

"Anything interesting?'' Joe asked when Frank came up for air.

"I want more than just one steroid box as evidence. If we can find a bunch, we have a much better case against Walsh."

Frank leaned into the next Dumpster and began digging through it rapidly. After a few moments he emerged with a small cardboard box full of empty steroid ampules. "Bingo! I hit the jackpot!" Frank said excitedly. "Look!" He pointed to Walsh's name and office address on the box, which also bore the return address of the manufacturer.

"That's great!" Joe replied. "I don't see how a legitimate doctor could be giving out steroids in this quantity."

Frank turned back to the Dumpster. "I want to see if I can find out who else Walsh is giving steroids to. Maybe I can find some old prescription forms or something."

He spent several minutes digging through the rest of the garbage before coming up with some dog-eared sheets of typing paper covered with names.

"What have you got now, Frank?" Joe asked.

"I think it's a list of Walsh's patients," Frank said after examining it.

"Look here," Frank said, indicating a note from Walsh scrawled in the margin that read: "Sue, please update the names and addresses of all current patients. J.W."

"Great work, Frank. Let's cross-check this

list of patients against a list of IWA wrestlers and see how many of them are seeing Walsh."

"My thinking exactly," Frank agreed. He looked up and down the alley. "If the coast is clear, let's get back to the van and go see Sammy."

As they drove to the training center, Joe turned to Frank and asked, "We know now that Walsh and Disaster are connected, but where do you think Missy fits in?"

"She's his manager, Joe. If Disaster's trying to kill Sammy, then Missy's probably involved, too."

"I sure hope not," Joe said bleakly.

When the Hardys returned to the IWA gym, they found a worried Sammy and Slim in the weight room.

"More trouble," Sammy greeted them.

"What happened now?" Joe asked.

"Sammy found a threatening note under the door of his dressing room when he came in this morning," Slim said glumly.

"Where is it?" Frank asked quickly.

"In my gym bag," replied Sammy.

Joe stepped over to Sammy's gym bag to retrieve the note. The note was hastily scribbled in pencil on coarse white paper.

It read: "Sammy Rand, if you make your speech on Saturday, you won't live to regret it. Don't make the speech! You have been warned!''

There was no signature, but a tiny grinning skull had been pasted to the bottom of the note.

"Do you think there's any point in showing this note to Warfield?'' Joe asked.

Sammy rolled his eyes. "You've talked to the man—what do you think? Every time I've mentioned anything to him about the threats, he just tells me I'm making them up for the publicity.''

"Maybe if we can show Warfield that a sizable number of IWA wrestlers are using Walsh's steroids, he'll get involved,'' Frank observed. "In the meantime, we can send out the note to have the handwriting analyzed.''

"I want you guys to stick close to me,'' Sammy told them. "I have a feeling that they're going to try something at tonight's bout.''

They went back to Sammy's dressing room, and Joe and Sammy cross-checked the list of Walsh's patients against a list of IWA wrestlers. Frank got on the phone to his father and arranged to have the handwriting in the note analyzed by an expert.

When he got off the phone, Frank found Joe and Sammy still poring over the list of Walsh's patients. They both looked deadly serious.

"We found at least six IWA wrestlers besides Disaster on Walsh's patient list," Joe told him.

"There's the Roman brothers, Baron Von Krupp, the Chain Gang tag team, and Pit Bull Parker," Sammy said.

"That's some roster," Frank commented. "Do you want to go to Warfield with this information?"

Sammy glanced at his watch. "It'll have to wait, Frank. I've got to rest for the match tonight. I'm still worn-out from yesterday."

That evening, as the trio drove up to the big covered arena, Frank noticed that the parking lot was filling up fast. Hordes of people were streaming through the main door of the arena, and the atmosphere was electric. People were milling about, obviously eager to see their favorite wrestlers in action.

Frank read the huge banner that hung over the entrance to the arena: IWA Wrestling Tonight! Sammy the "Kung Fu King" Rand vs. Tomahawk Smith. Major Disaster vs. Curious Cat. Tag-Team Action: The Romans vs. The Chain Gang.

Joe drove the van around to the entrance for wrestlers, and they all piled out.

Sammy went straight to the dressing room set aside for the good guys and quickly changed. Frank and Joe waited outside in the hallway. Frank scanned the bustling passage-way for any signs of danger, but he didn't sense any threat to Sammy among the wrestlers, managers, trainers, and reporters who streamed past.

Sammy emerged fifteen minutes later, clad in his wrestling costume. His gold lamé karate jacket gleamed under the fluorescent lights in the hallway. Sammy was smiling broadly, but Frank could tell that the big wrestler was nervous. A reporter, notebook in hand, came over to Sammy, but Slim waved him off. "See him after the match, huh, George?"

Joe noticed how worried Sammy was, too. "Don't worry about a thing, Sammy. Anybody who tries to get at you tonight will have to come through us first."

"Thanks, Joe. I'm glad you guys are around tonight."

The bout preceding Sammy's still had a few minutes remaining. Frank and Joe got the satisfaction of seeing Major Disaster being dropped to the floor in a full body slam. A few seconds later the Major was pinned. The Major got up and shook his fist at his opponent, vowing vengeance the next time they met.

"You're up, kid," Slim told Sammy.

"Let's do it," Sammy replied, and began walking down the aisle toward the ring.

The crowd roared as Sammy entered the arena. Frank saw that almost every person in the packed arena was standing and cheering as Sammy walked up the aisle.

A group of elderly women in outfits like Sammy's leaned over the barriers along the aisle to touch Sammy and wish him luck. Smiling, Sammy went over to the group, kissed some of them, and then continued on his way to the ring followed by Slim.

Smiling and waving with both hands, Sammy walked up to the ring, then climbed through the ropes that the referee held open for him. As he stepped into the center of the ring, the tuxedoed announcer grabbed a microphone suspended just over his head. His deep voice boomed over the arena's loudspeakers: "And now we proudly present the Heavyweight Champion of the IWA, Sammy the 'Kung Fu King' Rand!"

At this announcement the cheering from the crowd became even louder and more frenzied. Chants of "Sam-my! Sam-my!" rang out and echoed back and forth under the big domed roof.

The announcer next called out Tomahawk Smith's name as Sammy's challenger, and the tall wrestler stalked toward the ring from the bad guys' dressing room on the opposite side of the arena.

Frank saw that Smith's elaborate costume included fringed buckskin pants and a quill vest. Tomahawk gave a shrill cry and shook his tomahawk at the fans who were jeering him.

Glancing past Tomahawk, Frank suddenly noticed two oddly familiar faces in the crowd. He realized they were Daniel East and the Living Weapon. Frank wondered what they were doing there, then decided they must be checking out the competition.

Frank's attention was suddenly distracted from East and the Weapon by an ominous creaking sound. He looked around to find its source, and realized it was coming from above.

The creaking grew louder and louder. Frank looked up. The sound was coming from the huge, two-sided scoreboard that hung across the ring—it was hanging by only one corner!

Oblivious to the danger, Sammy was standing directly beneath the scoreboard, smiling and waving to his fans. In the next few seconds Sammy could be crushed!

Chapter

11

"SAMMY, WATCH OUT! The scoreboard's about to fall!" Frank ran to the edge of the ring.

The sound of screeching metal cut through the noise in the crowded arena. The audience's cheers had turned into screams. Joe looked up and saw the scoreboard swaying now by its single corner.

Joe immediately sprang into action. He, too, charged toward the ring. Joe knew that Sammy, the announcer, and the referee were in grave danger. They obviously didn't understand why everyone was screaming at them. The warnings must have sounded like just more noise.

In the next instant Frank slipped through

the ropes and physically knocked Sammy aside. They tumbled through the ropes.

Meanwhile, Joe had grabbed the referee and announcer and hauled them out of the ring.

A mere second after everyone was safe, the scoreboard tore loose. Frank cringed as the board slammed into the center of the ring, caving in a spot right where Sammy had been standing.

Joe stared at the scoreboard, which was sticking out of the canvas floor of the ring at a crazy angle. Then he glanced over at Sammy, who was sitting on the floor of the arena, cradling his right arm.

"Sammy, are you hurt?" asked Joe.

"No, not bad," Sammy replied, "but when Frank knocked me out of the way, I landed on my elbow. I think it's sprained."

The short, mustached referee appeared at the side of the ring. "Sammy, are you okay?"

Grimacing, Sammy shook his head. "Not really. It's my elbow. I can't wrestle tonight."

"The match is canceled anyway," the referee replied. "Nobody can wrestle in this mess," he said, gesturing toward the ring.

While Slim hovered anxiously in the background, Joe and Frank helped Sammy up and led him down the aisle. Joe noticed Stanley Warfield standing in front of the crowd.

"Still think Sammy's pulling publicity stunts, Mr. Warfield?"

"Nope," Warfield replied grimly, then he fell into step behind Sammy, Slim, and the Hardys.

Despite the pain he was in, Sammy managed to wave to the fans as he trudged up to the locker room door. The fans responded with loud cheering and applause.

Even before the Hardys got Sammy back to his dressing room, gray-uniformed maintenance men had begun to clear away the scoreboard.

Back in Sammy's dressing room Warfield took the Hardys aside while Dr. Towner and Slim examined Sammy's sprained elbow.

"Look, fellows," Warfield said, "I'm sorry I didn't believe you before about the attempts on Sammy. I'll do anything I can to help you catch the people responsible for these attacks."

"Thanks, Mr. Warfield," Frank said. "We'll let you know what you can do."

After Warfield left, Joe turned to Frank and shot him a questioning look. "Think we can trust him, Frank?" Joe asked in a low voice.

"Maybe, maybe not," Frank replied with a shrug. "We'll have to see how cooperative he is about protecting Sammy. In the meantime, let's check out the cables that held the scoreboard before the police get here."

"Sammy, can we leave you for a few minutes?" asked Joe.

"Sure, guys. I'll be okay. It's just a sprain—it

could have been a lot worse," Sammy said, taking a deep breath.

Frank and Joe left Sammy's dressing room and walked down the hall to a service elevator that went to the upper levels of the arena.

"These attacks on Sammy are getting more and more dangerous. A couple of seconds more and it would have been goodbye, Sammy," Frank said as the elevator doors slid shut.

Joe nodded. "Let's hope we can find some kind of a clue this time. So far we're just shooting in the dark."

They stepped out of the elevator, and Joe saw that a small maintenance catwalk had been lowered from the arena ceiling. Two electricians were working on a circuit breaker box on the other side of the dome. Joe and Frank walked around the curving gallery that hugged the arena wall just below the ceiling until they came to the end of the catwalk.

It swayed slightly when Joe took his first step on it, but it seemed sturdy enough. Joe and Frank moved cautiously out to the scoreboard's support cables, which were dangling from the center of the ceiling.

Joe grabbed the cable nearest him and examined the end. He saw that it had been partially sawed through—probably with a hacksaw.

"Frank, this one's been cut!" he said excitedly.

"So's this one!" Frank replied, examining the other cable. "Looks like it was sawed partway through, then gravity did the rest."

"Yeah, that's what I think," Joe echoed. "And whoever did this must be getting pretty desperate to stop Sammy. If that scoreboard had fallen slightly askew, it could have landed in the audience."

Frank stared down at the arena below. The disappointed fans were filing out through the exits. "That could have been a catastrophe. Who knows how many people would have been hurt.

"But what we have to keep in mind," Frank continued, "is that the scoreboard didn't land in the audience. Whoever did this knew exactly what he or she was doing. And that was to try to kill Sammy!"

The Hardys finished their examination of the cables and went back along the catwalk to the gallery just as the police flooded into the building. On the way back to the elevator Joe spotted something small and metallic gleaming on the floor.

"Hey, what's this?" he asked, bending over to pick it up. Holding it up to the light, he saw that it was a platinum lapel pin embossed with the logo of the East Broadcasting Corporation.

"What do you make of this, Frank?" Joe asked as he handed the pin to his brother.

Frank studied the pin. "EBC. Hmmm. Hey, I saw a pin just like this on East's lapel two days ago. We might be stuck with a new mystery here. These attacks on Sammy may not have anything to do with his antisteroid campaign."

"I don't follow you. Who else could be behind the attacks?"

"Daniel East, president of EBC," Frank said. "Remember what Sammy told us about East trying to get him to switch to the wrestling conference he broadcasts the meets for and the threats he made?"

"Oh, yeah!" Joe said, his face lighting up. "I got so involved in the steroid angle, I forgot that. Maybe these attacks are East's way of getting revenge on Sammy. Chet Morton told me that up until Sammy came along, the NAAW was bigger than the IWA."

"Maybe East is crazy enough or desperate enough to think that eliminating Sammy would put his wrestling conference back on top," Frank speculated.

"Let's go back to Sammy's place and show this pin to him," Frank said, heading for the elevator. "It's too late to visit the EBC now, but we can go there first thing in the morning."

"We should use our cover as young wrestlers to get in the door at the EBC," Joe suggested the next morning as they drove along the highway toward the EBC's headquarters.

Frank parked the van in front of a tall, black-glass office building. The sign on the lawn outside read East Broadcasting Corporation.

Inside the lobby of the building Frank scanned the directory. After a minute he determined that they should head to the fourth floor.

As soon as they stepped off the elevator, they were greeted by a pretty young receptionist who was sitting behind a sliding glass window.

"Hi, can I help you gentlemen?" she asked brightly.

"I sure hope so," Joe said, flashing his most charming smile. "We're wrestlers, and we'd like to speak with your wrestling programmer about signing on with the EBC."

"Wrestlers, huh?" The pretty receptionist smiled. "Who are you? Maybe I've heard of you."

"We're pretty new at the game," Frank answered, smiling. "I'm Frank Hardy, and this is my brother Joe. We call ourselves the, er, American Flyers."

"You'll want to speak to Miss Greta Yothers. I'll buzz her office and see if she's free." The receptionist spoke quietly into her phone, then told the Hardys, "She'll see you now.

Her office is the third one down on the right.''

"So far so good," Joe whispered as they walked toward Miss Yothers's office. The EBC offices hadn't been maintained very well for the past several years, Joe noted to himself. The walls needed painting and the carpeting was worn. Overhead, several fluorescent tubes had burned out and hadn't been replaced.

At Greta Yothers's office they knocked on the door. "Come on in," Joe heard a female voice call. The woman who asked them in was plump and in her late forties, with frosted blond hair and square-framed glasses.

"Hi, Miss Yothers, we're the American Flyers," Joe said, extending his hand to her.

"What can I do for you?" Greta Yothers replied, shaking hands with both of them.

"We were hoping the EBC would sign us on for their wrestling show," Frank quickly told her.

Miss Yothers's expression was very doubtful. "Well, business is a little slow right now, so we're sticking with proven commodities like the Living Weapon, Smash Bradley, and Firehouse Taylor."

"But wait till you get a load of our act," Joe insisted. He walked away from Frank a few steps, then faced him, holding his hands together in a stirrup at waist level. "Let's show her, Frank," Joe prompted. "Alley oop!"

Frank stepped back a pace, then ran forward, putting his left foot in Joe's joined hands. Joe smoothly tossed Frank up in the air, and he did a tight flip just below the ceiling.

But when he landed, Frank's foot slammed into a small coffee table, tipping it up and catapulting a heavy onyx ashtray through the air. It narrowly missed Miss Yothers's head, but it did crash through the window behind her.

"All right! I've seen enough! Get out of here!" she shouted angrily, pointing toward her door.

Miss Yothers furiously punched a button on her intercom. "Security!" she shouted into it. "Come to my office immediately!"

In seconds a broad-chested guard filled her doorway.

"Okay, let's go," the man said in a hard voice.

As Joe stepped out into the hall, he looked past the hulking security guard to the office at the end of the hall. A sign next to it identified it as Daniel East's office. The door was open and he could see East sitting behind his desk. East raised his eyes, and when he saw the Hardys he did a double take, and then he looked surprised.

It was obvious to Joe that East recognized

them. But why does he look so guilty? Joe wondered.

In the next instant the other two people in the room turned, too, and Joe saw they were the Roman brothers. They, too, were obviously shocked to see the Hardys.

"Let's go! Let's go!" the security guard shouted, pushing them down the hall.

As soon as the elevator door slid closed, Joe turned to his brother.

"Frank, did you notice East's expression?"

"Yes," Frank answered tightly. "He sure looked guilty."

"What do you think the Romans were doing there?" Joe asked. "I thought they had left East's wrestling conference to join the IWA."

"Maybe that's what we're supposed to think. Maybe the Romans are still working with East—undercover," Frank speculated.

"If the Romans are working for East, maybe they're the ones who've been trying to kill Sammy," Frank said as they stepped outside.

Passing a service alley next to the EBC building, Frank was suddenly grabbed and dragged into an alley. When Joe turned, he saw his brother struggling with a man in a ski mask.

But before Joe could even make a move to come to Frank's aid, a fist connected with his jaw. As Joe staggered around, he heard a gunshot echo deafeningly in the alley!

Chapter

12

THE BULLET MISSED Frank's ear by an inch. After it whizzed by, he shot out with his foot and knocked the gun out of the masked man's hand. He was on it in a second and kicked it behind a row of garbage cans.

The gunman didn't give up. He ran and butted his head into Frank's stomach, driving Frank back against the brick wall.

"Yow!" Frank cried, shaking his head to clear it. He countered with a karate chop to the gunman's neck.

"Oof!" the man grunted, but he quickly recovered to deliver a sharp punch to Frank's midsection again.

Frank momentarily lost his breath and doubled over in pain. The assailant moved in for the kill, and Frank waited for the perfect moment to raise an elbow and catch the masked man in his windpipe. The gunman dropped to the ground and lay there like a sack of potatoes.

"Well, that's one down," said Frank.

Frank checked Joe to see if he needed any help. Joe was struggling against another masked assailant, who had him immobilized in a headlock. Just as Frank stepped forward to come to his brother's aid, Joe stomped down hard on his opponent's instep and followed up with a quick karate chop to his side.

Howling with pain, the man released his grip on Joe, who immediately spun away. Then Joe's attacker turned to face Joe again.

Frank started off to help Joe, but was knocked off his feet by the recovered gunman. Frank smashed against the wall with his shoulder and soon felt himself sliding to the ground.

I guess he really wasn't out, Frank thought, reaching back to rub his shoulder in pain.

Seeing Frank on the ground, the gunman raised his foot to kick Frank in the face. But Frank shot out his hand and grabbed the guy's ankle. In an instant Frank pulled the thug's foot out from under him, and the man crashed to the ground, hitting his head.

"This time it doesn't look like you'll get up so quickly!" Frank said to his downed opponent.

Meanwhile, Joe's opponent looked over and

saw his partner on the ground. He left Joe and ran up to him. With strength and speed Joe hadn't thought possible, the thug scooped up his partner and sprinted down the alley toward the next street with his accomplice over his shoulder.

As Frank was getting up, Joe walked over and gave him a hand.

"Can you walk, Frank?" asked Joe.

Frank slowly brushed himself off. "Yeah, I'm okay," he said.

"Then let's go after them!" Joe insisted.

Joe ran down the alley at full speed after their attackers, with Frank following close on his heels.

Joe reached the mouth of the alley and checked in both directions down the next street. When Frank saw Joe punch the wall in frustration, he knew they had lost the two men.

Frank trotted up behind his brother. "No sign of them?"

"Nope. We lost them," replied Joe.

"Before we go back to the van and take care of our war wounds, let's find that gun," suggested Frank.

"Since those thugs got away, it might be the only clue we've got," replied Joe.

Remembering where he had kicked the gun, Frank led Joe back to the row of garbage cans. The Hardys began pulling them away from the alley wall until Joe spotted the gun on the ground.

"Got it!" Joe shouted as he scooped up the snub-nosed revolver.

"Has the serial number been filed off?" Frank asked.

"Nope," Joe replied, holding the gun out for Frank to examine.

"Great! This might be our first real break in this case," Frank said enthusiastically.

"Unless it's stolen," Joe pointed out. "Still, let's give it a try and call Dad with the serial number. Maybe he can track down the owner."

The cuts and bruises from their fight momentarily forgotten, the Hardys took off for their van.

"Are you sure, Dad?" Frank asked eagerly. "Great! Thanks a million. Yeah, we'll tell you all about it when we come home."

"Sounds like good news," Joe ventured.

"It is. Dad traced the serial number for us. It's registered to Daniel East, *and* it was never reported stolen."

"Well, now we have two pretty solid clues that connect East to this case," Joe said. "First we find an EBC lapel pin lying near the cut cables at the arena. Now we find out that the gun those two thugs tried to permanently silence us with belongs to him.

"I wouldn't be surprised if those two thugs we just fought were the Romans. They would have had time to get down here," Joe continued.

"Well, since those guys did get away, we don't know for sure, unfortunately," Frank pointed out. "Though their style of fighting did remind me of the Romans."

Frank was silent for a moment.

"Joe, do you remember when East showed up at the IWA gym with the Living Weapon?"

"Sure. Why?"

"We also saw the Weapon at the arena last night before the scoreboard fell. Since the Romans were wrestling, they couldn't have gotten to the scoreboard without attracting attention, so maybe the Weapon was the one who sabotaged the cables," Frank speculated.

"That makes sense," Joe agreed. "The Weapon's strong and fast enough to shinny up those cables and saw them partway through, then come back down and join East before the scoreboard falls."

"Our evidence definitely is pointing at East as the source of the attacks on Sammy," Frank concluded.

Joe nodded. "I agree. Now we need to know East's motive."

"Let's do a financial check on his company. It might be interesting to see how he's doing."

* * *

An hour later Frank was at his computer in Sammy's house, tapping into the network that supplied financial information on American companies for potential investors.

"Well, what kind of shape are East's holdings in?" Joe asked impatiently. "You know I can't read this stock market gibberish."

Frank smiled at his brother. "Wait a second and I'll call up an investor's newsletter that specializes in media companies. It ought to have a rundown on the performance of all of East's holdings for the last year or so."

Frank's fingers flew across the keyboard, and in moments dense columns of type scrolled down the screen. Both Hardys read in silence for several minutes, mentally digesting a large amount of information.

At length Joe broke the silence. "Frank, if I understand this correctly, both the EBC and the NAAW are on the verge of filing for bankruptcy. They're both heavily in debt.

"Remember how Sammy told us that East wanted to sell out to Warfield, and Warfield turned him down? I bet East plans on killing two birds with one stone. He gets revenge on Sammy for turning down an NAAW contract, and he eliminates him so he won't be overshadowing the NAAW wrestlers!"

Chapter

13

LATER THAT DAY, with Sammy working out at the IWA gym and Frank out, Joe thought Sammy's house was too quiet. But as he paced up and down Sammy's living room, he had to admit he was glad to have a little time to himself to sort out the flood of information they had unearthed in the last few days.

Just then the doorbell rang. Joe was surprised to find Stanley Warfield waiting on the front step.

"Mr. Warfield, what are you doing here?" Joe asked.

"I wanted to talk to you and your brother in private about these threats to Sammy."

"I'm glad you finally do believe the threats are real." Joe led Warfield into the living room.

Warfield shrugged. "I'm sorry I was so skeptical, but I've seen wrestlers pull every kind of stunt imaginable just to get publicity. One year Baron Von Krupp staged his own kidnapping to get on the front page of the papers. The FBI was called in, and it was a real mess."

Looking a little sheepish, Warfield added, "To be honest, this steroid campaign of Sammy's has been getting so much press, I felt as if he were stealing my thunder. Maybe that's why I was reluctant to take the threats seriously. Until that scoreboard fell," Warfield added, "I was sure Sammy was behind all this stuff.

"Sammy's pulled some wild publicity stunts, like the time he parachuted to a bout at the L.A. Coliseum, but I've never known him to do anything to endanger anyone's life."

"Well, the important thing is that you now believe someone's trying to kill Sammy," said Joe.

"That I do," Warfield agreed. "After thinking all night about the scoreboard incident, I'm convinced that someone is out to get him."

"Then we can really depend on your cooperation in clearing this up?" asked Joe.

Warfield nodded. "Absolutely. I'll do whatever I can to protect Sammy."

"Good. So far we've come up with a few suspects within the IWA—Major Disaster, Missy Mayflower, and the Romans," Joe replied.

"Disaster?" Warfield said in surprise. "I know there's no love lost between him and Sammy, but I never thought Fred would try to kill him."

"We've learned the Major's been arrested for attempted murder and has a prison record," Joe pointed out. "Did you know Disaster goes to a doctor who may be supplying him with steroids?"

"If the Major's using steroids, he'll be out. That's a pretty serious charge to make with no proof," Warfield said solemnly.

"We've got proof." Joe walked over to retrieve the steroid packages and Walsh's list of patients from the carton of evidence they'd collected so far. Also in the carton were the cassette, the damaged thermostat, the pistol, and the printouts of the information on East's companies, as well as Disaster's rap sheet and Missy's police record. Joe considered showing Warfield the other evidence, but a nagging doubt about Warfield's true motives made him cautious.

"This looks serious," Warfield agreed after examining the patient list and steroid box. "I want to get back to the office and contact the IWA board of directors about this. I'm sure they'll want to take some disciplinary action against Disaster. And while I'm at it, I'm going to contact the American Medical Association about this Dr. Walsh.''

Warfield shook hands with Joe, then let himself out.

Half an hour later Frank returned with a handwriting analysis of the threatening note. He was also carrying a pizza.

''What's the verdict on that note?'' Joe asked, hungrily digging into the pie.

''The analysts compared it with Disaster's signature on the rap sheet I sent them, and they say the handwritings are a match.''

''Well, this complicates things,'' Joe pointed out. ''Do you think Disaster's working with East?''

''No, I don't. I think East is behind the murder attempts on Sammy, with the Romans and maybe the Living Weapon helping him.

''We only have concrete proof linking Disaster to the threats against Sammy, not the murder attempts. It's possible he's just working with Walsh to make Sammy lay off steroid users.''

''So maybe your theory about Sammy being under attack from two groups at once is correct,'' Joe speculated. ''Maybe the threats and murder attempts are unrelated.''

''But we can't cross Missy off our list of

suspects just yet," Frank added. "Don't forget about the chair incident or the big knife you found in her purse. Sammy also saw her and Disaster near the sauna before he got roasted."

"I can't shake the feeling that those things are just circumstantial. I'm sure Missy is innocent," Joe said.

"Well, if you're that sure, then there's only one thing to do," Frank said. "Confront Missy directly with our evidence and get her story."

"I'm for that," Joe replied, wolfing down another slice of pizza. "It's pretty late now. Let's turn in and go see her tomorrow."

The next morning Sammy left early to tape a public service announcement against steroid use. He left a note for the Hardys saying that he'd meet them later at the gym. After a quick breakfast Frank and Joe headed over to the Mayflower mansion.

Joe steered the van through the wrought-iron gates and up the driveway, stopping near the front door.

The Hardys walked up the mansion's front steps, and Joe rang the ornate bell beside the front door. After a moment the front door was swung open by Missy.

"Hi, Joe," she said in a friendly voice. "What are you doing here?"

"I need to talk to you, Missy," he said seriously. "It's about all the accidents that have been happening to Sammy Rand."

"I don't care what happens to Sammy. He ruined my brother's career."

"Please, Missy," Joe said. "This is really important."

Missy stepped aside and ushered the Hardys inside. Joe briefly introduced Frank as Missy led them into the library.

"We can talk in here. Dad and Mitch are out back doing some skeet shooting," Missy explained.

Joe met her gaze and felt distinctly uncomfortable. "Well, I guess there's no nice way to ask this, but here goes. Have you had anything to do with any of Sammy's 'accidents'?"

"What? You mean that time with the chair?" Missy asked.

"That's one of the incidents," Frank put in. "Do you have an explanation for that?"

"Sure," Missy responded. "I didn't know the chair I gave the Major wasn't a breakaway. Victor Roman handed it to me."

"Oh, really?" said Joe.

"I had no idea Sammy was going to get hurt so badly. I felt awful about it, though I never said anything to Sammy because of the bad blood between us."

"Okay, that makes sense," Frank agreed. "But what about the knife Joe saw in your purse the night someone sawed through the climbing rope Sammy was using?"

Missy glared at Joe. "I wasn't aware that rifling through a lady's purse is among your habits. That's pretty sleazy."

"Ordinarily I don't. But I felt my friend's life was in danger," Joe explained.

Ignoring Joe, she stared at Frank.

"I can explain what the knife was doing in my purse. It's a birthday present for my dad for his weapons collection."

"But you and Disaster were in that room before the rope was cut," Frank pointed out.

"We weren't the last ones. The Romans were in there after us. Look, I'll take a lie detector test and swear that neither of us touched that rope," Missy stated. "We only ducked into that room for a few minutes to talk about business."

"There's something else about Disaster that needs to be addressed," Frank told her seriously. "Do you know he's been seeing a doctor who gives steroids to wrestlers?"

"Steroids?" Missy said in surprise. "I don't know anything about that."

"I talked to Stanley Warfield today, and he's checking into it," Joe said.

"We first suspected that you and Disaster might be involved in a vendetta against Sammy. Disaster because of his antisteroid campaign, and you because you hate him for hurting Mitch," Joe explained.

"If Warfield wants to clean up steroid use in the IWA, then I'm all for it, even if Sammy's spearheading the campaign," Missy said decisively.

"But what about the Major?" asked Joe.

"If he's violating IWA rules, then I won't help him," Missy replied. "Rules are rules. Let me know if there's anything I can do to help you protect Sammy. I don't know if I'll ever forgive him for hurting Mitch, but I'd like to make up for the chair incident."

"Thanks, Missy," Joe replied with a broad grin. "We'll tell Sammy you said that."

Frank stood up and went over to Missy. He shook hands with her. "And speaking of Sammy, Joe and I had better get over to the gym and check in with him."

Frank went over to the library doorway and turned to look at Joe, who was lingering over his goodbye to Missy. "Are you coming, Joe, or are you going to stay for dinner again?" asked Frank.

Half an hour later Frank and Joe found Sammy dripping with sweat as he practiced kicks and punches before a mirror. Joe noticed the bandage and tape around Sammy's elbow and saw that he was moving carefully, favoring his injured elbow.

"Hi, Sammy," Joe called as they walked over to him. "How's the elbow?"

Sammy stopped practicing and looked over at them. "It's a little sore, but I'm ready for tonight's bout with Disaster. Have you learned anything?"

"Plenty," Frank replied. "Like for instance, Daniel East is going broke."

"No kidding," Sammy replied. "I knew the IWA was clobbering him in the ratings, but I didn't think he was that bad off."

"He didn't used to be," Frank told him. "But I did a little digging into his finances and learned that the decline of EBC and the NAAW coincided with your stardom and the rise of the IWA."

"Do you think East blames me for his problems?" Sammy asked. "Is he after me because I wouldn't join the NAAW?"

"It's starting to look that way," Joe answered. "We also think the Romans might still be working for East. We saw them at the EBC offices yesterday."

"And right after we left there, we got jumped by two guys who definitely knew how to wrestle," Frank added.

Sammy looked thoughtful as he wiped the sweat from his face. "Come to think of it, I heard the Romans' trainer complaining that they'd missed a training session yesterday."

"That's one more piece of circumstantial

evidence against the Romans,'' Joe commented.

Sammy turned away from the mirror. "Guys, I want to hear everything you've dug up so far, but I have to keep working out to keep my elbow from getting stiff. How about working out with me while we talk?''

"Sounds good, Sammy. We'll just go and get changed.'' Joe and Frank headed for the equipment room.

Joe stepped through the door of the equipment room to look for Slim or one of the other trainers.

The door to the back office in the equipment room was open, so Joe led his brother toward it.

They made their way down a narrow aisle between two racks of training gear toward the office. But as they neared the door, Joe felt himself being grabbed from the side by strong hands.

He struggled unsuccessfully against the unseen enemy and felt a wet cloth being pressed over his mouth and nose. The last thing he was aware of as he lost consciousness was the sickly sweet odor of chloroform filling his nostrils.

Chapter

14

FRANK RETURNED to consciousness with a splitting headache. He tried to open his eyes but soon realized that he had been blindfolded and gagged. He also tried to move his hands, but they had been securely tied behind his back. He took a deep breath and started to adjust to his surroundings.

Frank felt something warm resting against his back and knew it must be Joe. He heard muffled noises that sounded as if Joe was trying to speak with a gag in his mouth. He could feel Joe struggling and knew he was tied up, also.

Both of them were rocking back and forth where they lay, and Frank guessed that they were shut up in the back of a moving vehicle.

After what seemed like forever, the vehicle lurched to a stop, and Frank heard doors slamming. A moment later he heard another set of doors open and could sense light streaming in on him.

Frank's heart was racing and sweat was pouring down his face. What do these people want from us? he thought. In the next instant he was picked up and roughly slung over someone's shoulder. I'd better relax, he told himself, so they'll think I'm still unconscious. Frank was carried a short distance before he was dropped on the floor of a dark room. A moment later he heard a heavy thud that he assumed was Joe being dropped beside him on the floor. Then he heard a door shut and a bolt thrown.

Frank knew he had to come up with a quick plan to free himself and Joe. He rolled from side to side until he was lying facedown on the floor. He scraped the lower part of his face along the wooden floorboards until he felt the tape come loose on his mouth.

He lay in that position for a moment, breathing hard, his face sore from the scrapes.

"We've got to get out of here, Joe," Frank whispered. "Can you move your hands?"

"Uh-huh," he heard Joe grunt.

"Good," Frank answered. "I'll roll over to you and try to put my hands next to yours.

See if you can loosen the ropes around my hands."

Joe grunted affirmatively again.

Frank rolled onto his side again and bumped toward the sound of Joe's voice. After a moment his back nudged against Joe's. He felt Joe struggling to get up on his side and groped blindly for Joe's hands.

To Frank's great relief, he soon felt one of Joe's hand in his own and pulled it toward his back. Frank lay on his side for what seemed like an eternity while Joe fumbled with the ropes tied around his brother's wrists. Just as Frank began to feel his arm going numb, he felt a knot loosen. He strained against his bonds and felt his left hand slip free.

"Way to go, Joe!" Frank whispered triumphantly.

Pushing himself over on his chest with his free hand, Frank got off his sore right arm and flexed it to start the circulation. Then he quickly pulled the ropes from his wrist and whipped off his blindfold.

He strained his eyes, trying to get a look at the room they were in. In the dim light that filtered under the door of the windowless room, Frank could see they were in an empty storeroom.

Next he turned his attention to untying Joe. His fingers felt clumsy after being immobilized, but he did free Joe's hands in a few minutes.

As soon as his hands were free, Joe pulled the gag off his mouth and tore off his blindfold.

"How do you feel?" Frank asked as he stood up and stretched his stiff muscles.

"Like garbage," Joe replied, massaging his arms. "That chloroform gave me a massive headache."

"Me, too," Frank admitted. "But at least neither of us is seriously hurt."

"Not yet, but what happens when our playmates decide to come back and finish us off?"

"I hope we'll be out of here before that happens," replied Frank. "Speaking of which, let's find a way out of here, pronto."

Joe stood up and, after stretching his arms, began examining the door and walls.

"I heard a bolt being thrown after they dropped us in here," Joe observed. "And the hinges are on the outside of the door, so we probably can't get out that way."

Frank walked over to the wall, and ran his fingers over it, looking for any kind of opening, but the walls were bare. Then suddenly his hands hit a grille set high up in the wall opposite the doorway.

"Hey, Joe, here's something!" Frank whispered excitedly. "It's an air-conditioning grille. And it feels wide enough to crawl through."

"Great!" Joe whispered. "But how are we going to get it off the wall?"

Frank felt around in his pockets for a moment. All he found was some loose change.

"It feels like a dime would fit into the slots in the screwheads. Do you have a dime?"

"I think so," Joe answered, and handed Frank a dime.

Wasting no time, Frank and Joe began removing the screws that held the corners of the grille in place. It was hard work and Frank's wrist ached by the time he felt the last screw come loose.

"Quietly now," he cautioned Joe as they pulled the grille from the wall.

They set the grille on the floor as silently as possible, then Frank put his hands on the edge of the air-conditioning duct and chinned himself up into it. It was a tight fit, but Frank was able to crawl forward at a moderate pace. He heard Joe clambering up behind him.

"Where to now, Frank?" he heard Joe whisper behind him.

"Wherever this takes us. I don't think we have much choice," Frank said.

"Lead on," Joe replied in a hoarse whisper.

Frank crawled forward about thirty feet and came to a junction of two ducts. He thought he heard the faint sound of voices to his right, so he crawled in that direction. He'd like to be able to identify his kidnappers for the police. He continued on for another fifty feet. The sound of the voices grew louder and louder.

He finally came to a grille with light streaming through. As he approached it, he could hear talking and the sounds of people moving around below. He crawled over to the grille and peered through it.

Below him Frank could see a table with an automatic shotgun and boxes of ammunition resting on it. Frank also saw several wrestling boots, a spool of thread, and some small bottles that looked as if they contained medicine of some kind.

He crawled up a little farther and was able to see more of the room. He froze when he saw Victor Roman standing by the table. Frank peered around the room and also made out Jimmy Roman and the Living Weapon.

Frank couldn't see him, but suddenly he heard Daniel East's nasal voice saying, "So, what do you think of our little booby trap, Victor?"

"Cute." Victor smirked, picking up one of the wrestling boots from the table. "But are you sure it'll work on Sammy?"

"Since he's wrestling Major Disaster tonight, it's a cinch. I've seen Disaster wrestle maybe forty times. He always uses the flying dropkick move. Always!" Frank identified that speaker as the Living Weapon.

Frank saw Victor turn the boot upside down and press his thumb into the heel. A sharp silver needle popped from the heel.

"Hey, Victor, be careful with that thing, or you'll get a dose of that heart attack drug," Frank heard Jimmy Roman caution his brother.

"I'm being careful," Victor shot back. "Stop being such a worrywart, Jimmy."

"You really should be cautious how you handle that thing," East told him. "A few drops of heart stimulant can induce a massive heart attack."

"But what if they do an autopsy on Sammy?" Victor asked. "Won't they find the drug in his body?"

"No," East replied, chuckling nastily. "That's the beauty of this stuff. It breaks down very quickly in the bloodstream. It's practically untraceable unless you know what to look for. And when Sammy dies, it'll just look like he had a heart attack.

"The boot with the poisoned needle is already in Disaster's locker at the arena. So, very shortly after he steps into the ring, it's goodbye to the Kung Fu King."

Frank felt a surge of anger when he realized the fate East and his cronies had in store for Sammy. Frank silently beckoned to Joe to follow him.

They kept crawling until they came to another branch in the ductwork. Frank crawled to his left until he came to another grille that looked out on a wide empty room. He rolled over on his back and braced his feet against the grille. Frank shoved hard and felt the grille loosen. He gave it a hard kick with both feet and felt the bottom of the grille pop out from the wall as the screws went flying. He quickly wormed his way back to the opening and crawled through, hoping East and the others hadn't heard the noise.

After dropping to the floor, Frank stood up and helped Joe crawl out of the opening. Then when Joe was out, Frank turned around to see where he was.

Frank saw that they stood against one wall of a large, mostly empty warehouse that contained only a blue sedan, a big black Lincoln Continental, and a white paneled van.

Against the far wall of the warehouse Frank noticed several glassed-in offices. He could make out East and the Romans in one of them.

There was a row of fifty-gallon drums near the wall, and Frank ducked behind them, with Joe quickly following his example. Frank peered over the top of the row of drums and saw East open a small leather shoulder bag and brandish a compact Ingram Mac-10 machine gun.

He grabbed Joe's shoulder and pointed at

it. Joe nodded, indicating that he had seen it, too.

Joe leaned over to Frank's ear and whispered, "This is getting out of hand, Frank. Let's call the cops on these dirtbags right now."

"We've seen and heard enough to put them all away," Frank agreed. "But in order to call the cops, we have to get out of here!"

Frank scanned the inside of the warehouse for an exit. Finally his eyes fell on a pay phone at the far end of the building.

"Joe, I don't see an exit, but there's a phone down there! I'm going to try to sneak down and phone the police," whispered Frank.

"Okay, but stay low and out of sight," Joe warned him.

Frank crouched and ran toward the phone, using whatever cover would shield him from East and the others.

Frank's heart was pounding when he reached the phone. He punched in 911 and heard a guttural voice announce, "Bethlehem P.D. How may I help you?"

"I've got an emergency, officer. My name's Frank Hardy. I've been kidnapped, and my kidnappers are planning to murder someone later tonight. If you send some squad cars over right now, you can bag the whole gang."

"Where are you, Mr. Hardy?" the voice asked.

Frank felt a sudden flash of panic. "I don't know! I was blindfolded when I was brought here."

Frank looked at the pay phone and got an inspiration. "Wait a minute. If I tell you the number where I'm calling from, can you find this place? It's a big warehouse somewhere in Bethlehem."

Static crackled over the line as the anonymous cop pondered Frank's request.

To his relief, the cop answered, "Yeah, that's no problem. What's the number, Mr. Hardy?"

Reading it off the front of the phone, Frank told the cop, "The number's 555-9997. Hurry, please!"

"We're on our wa—" the cop began, then the line fell silent.

"Hello? Hello?" Frank whispered, frantically tapping the switch hook.

"It's too late for that, kid," an angry voice rasped from somewhere to Frank's left. He whirled around and saw the Living Weapon standing there with a bundle of severed phone wires in one hand and a gleaming military combat knife in the other.

The Weapon dropped the wires and moved toward Frank, the long knife pointed at his heart.

Chapter

15

FROM HIS HIDING PLACE behind a row of rusting fifty-gallon drums, Joe watched the Living Weapon advance on Frank with a drawn knife.

Joe frantically searched around for some weapon he could use to stop the hulking wrestler before he reached Frank. Raising his eyes, he spied a block and tackle dangling by a rusty chain from an overhead beam.

Joe jumped up on a packing crate below the block and tackle, then leapt high and grabbed it. The block and tackle swayed when Joe put his weight on it. Joe added to his momentum by pumping his legs back and forth. He swung backward into the wall, grabbed a metal bracket jutting from the side of the wall, and hung there for a split second.

Joe let go of the bracket and swung forward, straight toward the Living Weapon, who was backing Frank into the wall.

"Yaaaaa!" Joe screamed as he swung down on the Weapon. The wrestler turned around just as Joe's feet connected with his chest, sending him tumbling backward.

The Weapon landed heavily, and his knife went flying off behind a pile of rusty compressors.

"Frank—run for the exit! Straight ahead!" Joe shouted as he landed on all fours.

Frank wasted no time following his brother's advice. He sprinted for the huge double doors, with Joe only a few steps behind him.

But although the Weapon was down, he wasn't out. Behind them, Joe heard the Weapon shout, "Dan! Victor! Jimmy! The kids are getting away! Stop them!"

Joe risked a glance over at the office where East and the Romans were. He saw all three of them appear in the doorway with weapons. Jimmy Roman leveled a pistol at them, but East grabbed his arm and pulled it up.

"No shooting!" East snarled. "Do you want to bring the cops down on us?"

Jimmy jammed the pistol into the waistband of his pants and charged after the Hardys. Joe noticed that Victor was not slow to follow his younger brother.

Joe saw Frank reach the big double doors.

He grabbed a door handle and threw his shoulder into it, shoving it slowly back along its track. Joe was there several seconds later, throwing his weight into helping to move the heavy door.

As soon as they pushed the doors open wide enough to squeeze through, the Romans arrived.

Jimmy grabbed Joe by the shoulder and spun him around. He threw a savage roundhouse punch, which Joe successfully ducked. Out of the corner of one eye, Joe saw Victor leap on Frank, knocking him to the ground.

Jimmy threw a hard left at Joe's face, which Joe knocked away with a forearm block. Joe countered with a straight punch to Jimmy's midsection, which caught him off guard and sent him reeling backward.

Joe kept up a barrage of punches, driving Jimmy back more. The dark-haired wrestler's heels caught in a deep groove in the pavement, and he fell flat on his back.

Suddenly Joe heard an approaching police siren cut the air. "All right! Just in time!" he exulted.

His exultation was short-lived, however, for he saw East and the Living Weapon run to some windows at the front of the building. East carried the Ingram Mac-10 Joe had seen earlier. The Weapon carried a folding stock automatic shotgun.

The two gunmen smashed out the windows and peered over the sill, holding their guns at the ready.

Joe looked around for Frank and saw that Victor Roman had gotten the upper hand. Victor had Frank down on the ground and was twisting his arm behind his back.

Joe got up to go to Frank's aid, but the Living Weapon suddenly noticed the movement and snapped off a shot at Joe. The shower of shotgun pellets missed by inches as Joe dived for the pavement. He looked over at the Weapon, but he and East were concentrating on the police and could spare no more attention for the Hardys.

Joe glanced over at Frank, who was struggling to escape the arm bar Victor had him in. Joe saw Frank blindly grope for a piece of scrap metal that was lying on the floor.

With a desperate heave, Frank swung his arm and smashed the metal piece down on Victor's foot. Howling with pain, Victor released his grip on Frank's arm and danced around holding his injured foot.

"Frank—his glass jaw!" Joe shouted.

Joe saw Frank walk over to Victor and deliver a solid right to the jaw. Victor fell to the warehouse floor.

Joe heard more police cars arrive. He looked over toward East and the Weapon, and saw them let off a few rounds at the police.

The police returned fire, and Joe ducked for cover behind the white panel van. Frank joined him a moment later, panting from exertion. "There's not much we can do now without risking a bullet!" Joe shouted over the din of sirens and gunshots.

"I agree," Frank shouted back. "Let's let the cops handle this!"

The gunfire within the warehouse suddenly ceased, causing Joe and Frank to trade questioning looks. Joe crawled around the rear of the van to see what East and the Weapon were doing.

"More cops!" East shouted in frustration.

"There's too many to fight!" the Weapon called back. "Let's blow this joint before we're surrounded!"

East looked uneasily out the window, then jumped back as the cops fired at him. He stepped back against the wall beside the window and dropped the spent magazine from his machine gun.

"You start up the Lincoln!" he commanded. "I'll lay down covering fire to keep them off our backs!"

The Weapon nodded, then sprinted over to the big black Lincoln Continental. He dived behind the wheel, and a moment later its powerful engine roared to life.

East fired two long bursts from his powerful gun, then ran frantically for the Lincoln. Even before he had closed the door, the Living Weapon had thrown the car into gear and was roaring toward the rear door of the warehouse.

"Those maniacs! They're going to smash through the door!" Joe shouted in amazement.

"I think that's exactly what they have in mind," Frank agreed a moment before the big car hurtled through the outer wall of the warehouse in a shower of splinters and glass.

The cops kept shooting at the window where East had stood.

"Somebody better stop the shooting," Frank suggested.

"You go," Joe told him. "I'll make sure the Romans don't get away before the cops come in."

Frank gingerly edged over to a window and waved a white handkerchief at the police. Meanwhile, Joe took down a canvas fire hose and tied up the Romans.

A moment later a pair of cops carrying pump shotguns came through the door, their weapons at the ready.

"Don't shoot, officers! We're the ones who called you!" Frank shouted, holding his hands up.

"Where're the creeps with the heavy artillery?" a tall cop with a booming voice asked.

"They went thataway!" Joe told him, pointing at the gaping hole in the rear door of the warehouse.

"They were driving a black Lincoln Continental hardtop."

"Did you get the license number?" the tall cop asked.

Joe shook his head. "Sorry, there was too much going on."

"I did, officer," Frank said calmly as he joined Joe. "It was GRA one-nineteen."

"Thanks kid," the tall cop replied. "Dudley, you call that in while I check this place out," he told his partner.

The shorter officer nodded his head once and trotted off.

"You two kids stay here!" the tall cop ordered. Then he walked over to the glassed-in offices on the opposite side of the warehouse.

Joe suddenly grabbed Frank's arm to look at his watch. "Frank, look at the time!"

Frank's watch read 8:05. With a feeling of dread, Joe realized that Sammy's fatal bout with Major Disaster had already begun.

"We've got to get out of here!" Joe said urgently.

"Joe, the cops aren't going to let us go before questioning us," Frank reminded him.

"Then we'll have to make a break for it," said Joe. "Out the back the way East went."

Keeping an eye on the cop checking the offices, Joe led Frank to the van.

"You get the van started, Frank," Joe ordered. "I'll stay outside to distract them if

I have to. Leave the side door open, and I'll jump in at the last minute.''

"What if there are no keys in the van?'' Frank asked.

"Then hotwire it. Just do it! Sammy's life may depend on it.''

Giving his younger brother an I-hope-you-know-what-you're-doing look, Frank sneaked over to the van and climbed in. He cranked the engine on and spun the van backward and in a circle so it faced the rear opening. He hit the gas, and the van shot forward. As it passed Joe, he leapt in through the side door.

"Hey—'' Frank heard the tall cop shout from the far end of the warehouse.

As the van roared out of the warehouse, Frank checked the rearview mirror and saw the tall officer draw and raise his pistol. Then he heard him shout, "Stop. Stop or I'll shoot!''

Chapter

16

FRANK'S HEART was in his throat as the van screeched up to the arena. Even though he had made great time, Frank knew Sammy's match was already under way. He glanced at his watch. It now read 8:19.

Sammy could already be dead from the effects of the heart drug on the needle concealed in Disaster's boot.

Frank felt as if he were moving through molasses as he and Joe pushed through the boisterous crowds of wrestling fans clogging all the entrances to the main ring.

Joe's expression was worried when he turned to Frank. "I don't think we're going to make it in time!" he shouted over the screaming of the crowd.

"Keep pushing!" Frank shouted back. "Sammy's life may be riding on what we do next!"

Frank and Joe pushed and squirmed through hordes of wrestling fans, all wearing T-shirts bearing the names and faces of their favorite grapplers, or in some cases even dressing like their favorites. Finally they made it to the interior of the arena. Frank stood on tiptoe to peer over the heads of the crowd and saw that Sammy was still alive. He and Major Disaster were circling each other, each looking for an opening to strike.

"Sammy's still alive, Joe!" Frank shouted excitedly.

"Then let's keep him that way!" Joe yelled, pushing through a group of Major Disaster fans dressed in Disaster's trademark khaki muscle T-shirt, crisscrossed with bandoliers of machine-gun cartridges.

"Hey, watch where you're going!" a fat Disaster fan with a camouflage headband snarled at Joe.

"Sorry, but it's an emergency!" Frank called over his shoulder as he followed in Joe's wake through the rowdy crowd.

"Hey—come back here!" the fat man shouted at Joe's and Frank's backs as they pushed their way to the edge of the ring.

Major Disaster climbed up on the ropes and was preparing to spring in a flying drop kick. But just before he could make his move, Joe charged up behind him and locked both arms around Disaster's waist.

Across the ring Sammy's jaw dropped in surprise. "Joe, what—" he sputtered.

"Sammy, get out of the ring!" Joe cut him off. "Get out before Disaster kills you!"

Missy Mayflower, dressed in a low-cut royal blue evening gown and matching feather boa, rose from where she was sitting at ringside with Stan Warfield.

"No! Joe, get out of the ring!" Missy screamed.

"We can explai—" Frank started to say, but Missy was charging Joe, brandishing one of her royal blue high-heel shoes like a weapon.

Frank intercepted her, lifting her up by her waist.

"Put me down!" Missy shrieked, kicking and flailing around. She struggled so hard that Frank almost dropped her.

All around the arena, Frank heard loud booing and shouts of "Unfair!" erupt from Major Disaster's fans.

Frank shouted at the top of his voice to make himself heard over Missy's shrieking and the crowd's noise. "Sammy—get out of the ring! Listen to Joe! You're in danger!"

Sammy looked very confused and backed away from Disaster. This move prompted Disaster's fans to boo even louder and shout

"Chicken!" and "Coward!" at Sammy. Some of them even hurled popcorn bags and soda cups at the bewildered champion. Sammy's fans rallied to his defense, and a number of fistfights erupted between fans of the two wrestlers.

Sammy stepped through the ropes and walked toward Frank.

"Sammy, you yellowbelly—come back here and fight!" Disaster snarled, struggling to break Joe's grasp.

When Sammy left the ring, Disaster growled at Joe, "Kid, when I get loose I'll murder you and your brother, too!"

"I don't suppose it would help if I explained why we're doing this," Joe said through gritted teeth.

Suddenly Disaster drove both elbows back into Joe's arms, which stunned Joe and caused him to loosen his grip. It was all Disaster needed. He grabbed Joe's hands and pulled them apart, then jumped away from the ropes. Disaster was moving so quickly, Joe didn't have time to react. Disaster grabbed Joe's arms and yanked him over the top rope, hurling him to the far side of the ring. Ecstatic cheering erupted from Disaster's fans when he did this. "Kill him, Major!" a female voice shouted. And a rhythmic chant of "Drop kick! Drop kick!" started up.

Joe tried to roll when he landed, but it hurt

him. Shaking his head to clear it, Joe tried to rise. Disaster pounced on him, knocking Joe to the mat with an ax-handle blow to his back.

Next, Disaster picked Joe up to raise him overhead for a full body slam. But before he dropped Joe, Disaster turned to Frank and snarled, "You're next, punk!"

Shoving Missy into the startled Sammy's arms, Frank said, "Hang on to this wildcat, Sammy!"

Before Sammy had a chance to object, he was hanging on to Missy, trying to keep her from smacking him on the head with her shoe.

In the next instant Frank launched himself into the air, slamming into Disaster's midsection with a body block. A chorus of boos rained down from Disaster's fans.

Disaster fell like a collapsing house of cards, with Joe on top of him. Frank put all his weight on Disaster's legs, holding them to the mat.

Major Disaster growled and thrashed, but he was unable to dislodge the Hardys.

To Frank's surprise, he saw the perplexed-looking referee get down on the mat next to them and make a count of three.

When the Hardys didn't immediately release Major Disaster, the referee indicated that they should get up, saying, "The match is over. You two won."

Frank got off Disaster's legs while Joe

untwined his arms and legs from Disaster's arms. They stood up together, and the referee grabbed Joe's left hand and Frank's right hand and held them up in the air.

"I hereby declare—" He paused and whispered to them from the corner of his mouth, "Quick, what are your names?"

"Frank and Joe Hardy," Frank whispered back.

"I hereby declare Frank and Joe Hardy the winners of this bout," the ref said with a smile. Disaster's fans booed and hurled trash at the Hardys. "Hey, what can I do, folks?" the ref said. "They pinned him!"

"I demand a new match!" Major Disaster shouted angrily. "This wasn't supposed to be a tag-team bout, or I would've brought a partner!"

"Take it easy, Major," Sammy told him as he put Missy down and stepped through the ropes into the ring. "I'm sure the Hardys have a good reason for what they did."

"Garbage!" Missy shot back. "I bet you put them up to it, Sammy!"

"Yeah," Disaster growled. "You can't beat me fairly, so you use kids!"

"Sorry we had to horn in on your bout, Major," Frank told him, turning away from the referee. "But we had to stop you before you killed Sammy with your flying drop kick.

You were being set up as the fall guy in a plan to murder Sammy.''

"What?" Disaster said in surprise.

"What's going on here?" Stanley Warfield suddenly shouted from the edge of the ring. "I thought you guys were investigating the threats against Sammy, not trying to break into wrestling."

"I demand to know what's going on," Missy Mayflower shouted from beside Warfield.

"This is going to take a lot of explaining," said Frank.

"Yeah, but first we need to talk to the Major in private," Joe put in.

"If you're going to interrogate him, then I demand to be there!" Missy insisted.

Joe and Frank exchanged looks, then nodded.

"Okay," Frank agreed. "That's reasonable."

A few moments later Missy ushered the Hardys into Major Disaster's dressing room, where the Major waited for them wearing a sullen expression.

"What's this about?" Missy asked as soon as Frank and Joe closed the door behind them.

"We have proof that the Major was the one threatening Sammy with notes and phone calls," Joe told her.

"What proof?" Disaster snarled.

"A note in your handwriting, for one thing,"

Frank explained, adding, "And a taped phone threat that could be matched with your voice print even though you tried to disguise your voice."

"Look, if you cooperate, it'll make things easier," said Joe.

Disaster glared defiantly at the Hardys for a moment, then dropped his eyes. "Okay, I guess you're right. What do you want to know?"

"Why were you threatening Sammy?" Frank asked.

"Dr. Walsh was blackmailing me. He threatened to tell Warfield and the wrestling press that I used steroids unless I shut Sammy up. Walsh was afraid Sammy's antisteroid campaign would ruin his business of supplying steroids to wrestlers."

"What about the attacks on Sammy?" Joe asked. "The cut rope, the chair, the ammonia in the water bottle?"

"Not to mention the falling scoreboard and Sammy's getting locked in the sauna," Frank added.

Disaster's eyes widened. "I didn't have anything to do with that stuff, I swear!"

"Tell them the truth, Fred," Missy ordered.

"I *am* telling the truth, Missy! I swear on my mother's grave!" Disaster pleaded.

Missy looked over at the Hardys. "Can you

leave us alone, guys? I need to talk to Fred in private."

"Sure, Missy," Joe replied. "Come on, Frank."

"We'll be in Sammy's dressing room," Frank told her, then turned to Disaster and said, "Major, we'll need your wrestling boots before we go."

Disaster took them off and handed them to Frank without a word.

Frank and Joe joined Sammy and Warfield in Sammy's dressing room, where Frank set the boots on Sammy's makeup counter.

"Those are the Major's boots. Do you mind telling me what this is about?" Warfield asked sternly.

"Major Disaster was being set up by Daniel East to kill Sammy in the ring tonight," Frank explained.

"What do his boots have to do with that?" Warfield asked testily.

"I'll show you," Frank explained, picking up the right boot and pressing a spot near the center of the heel. Joe couldn't help noticing Warfield's look of surprise and Sammy's shocked expression when a needle popped out of the boot.

"That needle is coated with a drug that would have induced a heart attack," Frank told Warfield and Sammy. "East, the Romans, and the Living Weapon kidnapped us from the

IWA gym. But we escaped and overheard East explaining his plan to the Romans.''

Sammy clutched his throat and turned white.

"Your success with the IWA was driving East Broadcasting and the NAAW out of business," Frank told him.

"That's what all those attempts on your life were about, Sammy," Joe continued. "Our guess is that East thought that eliminating you would improve his own fortunes. He had the Romans and the Living Weapon helping him. Since you ran into Victor Roman coming out of the sauna, I'm sure he and his brother were the ones who rigged the thermostat and locked you in.''

"And who were those two goons who jumped you in the alley?" Sammy asked.

"The Romans," Joe answered. "It had to be them because of their fighting style and because they saw us at EBC when we went there.''

"But who did all that other stuff to me?" Sammy asked.

"We're sure it was the Romans and, in some cases, the Living Weapon, acting under East's orders," Frank told him. "Missy said that Victor Roman handed her the chair that Disaster hit you with. She also saw the Romans coming out of the workout room just before we discovered the rope was cut. So they had to be the ones who did it. One of the Romans put the ammonia in your water bottle, since neither East nor the Weapon was seen in the gym that day."

"The Living Weapon had to be the one who cut the scoreboard cables," Joe put in. "But East had to have helped him because of the lapel pin we found."

"So who was threatening to stop me from making my speech?" Sammy asked.

"I can answer that," Frank cut in. "Disaster. He wasn't trying to kill you, but he sure was behind those threats."

"Do you have proof of that?" Warfield asked.

"Solid proof," Frank replied. "The handwriting in the last note threatening Sammy matches Disaster's handwriting exactly."

"Well, if Disaster wasn't working with East, what was he after?" Sammy wanted to know.

"Dr. Walsh was blackmailing him to stop your antisteroid speech. Walsh threatened to expose Disaster's own steroid use and get him thrown out of the IWA."

There was a knock on the door, and Missy appeared in the doorway.

"Mr. Warfield, I've talked with the Major, and he's prepared to testify that Dr. Jacob Walsh gave him steroids illegally. He also offered to point out the other steroid users in the IWA."

"Well, if Major Disaster's willing to cooperate, maybe he'll be allowed back in the game eventually. He'll have to be banned for a while, though," Warfield said.

Suddenly the phone in Sammy's dressing room rang. Sammy answered it, then handed it to Warfield, telling him, "It's for you, Stan."

Warfield grabbed the phone and said, "This is Warfield. Yeah? Uh-huh, uh-huh. Well, that's certainly good news."

He hung up the phone, telling Sammy and the Hardys, "That was a friend of mine in the Allentown P.D. The Bethlehem cops captured East and the Living Weapon about fifteen minutes ago. The Weapon's making a full confession in exchange for leniency. They have Daniel East and the Romans cold."

"All right!" Joe said. He turned to Frank and slapped him a high five. Frank slapped back.

"Looks like everything's pretty well wrapped up," Joe said, grinning broadly.

"I want to apologize to you, Joe," Missy said sweetly. "You guys did the right thing."

"Now that we've solved this mystery, how about going out with me tonight?" Joe asked, turning on the charm.

Missy reached over and squeezed his arm briefly. "Joe, I'd love to, but since the Major's going to be out of action for a while, I need a new wrestler to manage. I'm going to try to talk Tomahawk Smith into letting me manage him.''

Frank couldn't help smiling at the crestfallen expression on Joe's face after Missy left. He went over to his younger brother and clapped him on the back. "Don't take it so hard, Joe. Maybe you can still get her if you come up with a good enough costume."

"Yeah!" Joe said, his eyes lighting up. "Got any ideas?"

"Well," Frank said, carefully moving out of his brother's reach. "How about something, say, in powder blue? It always was your best color!"

Frank and Joe's next case:

Historian Andrew Donnell invites the Hardys to Tennessee to join in a reenactment of the battle of Shiloh—Frank in Confederate gray, Joe in Union blue. But soon both boys are seeing red. Rifles are raised, shots ring out, and Donnell falls to the ground—cut down by real bullets!

The Hardys check out the nearby Civil War theme park, where their fun soon turns to terror. The tunnel of love, the hall of mirrors, and the Rebel Yell roller coaster have been rigged to thrill the boys to death. The war games are over, the true battle has begun—and Frank and Joe are directly in the line of fire . . . in *Uncivil War*, Case #52 in The Hardy Boys Casefiles™.